its tail satisfactorily erect. The two had to retreat suddenly to the doorstep where Hughie sat, so impetuous it grew. Hughie was not, like the others, at home because he was too small to go to school. Indeed, no! Hughie was ten, and at home to-day because he had been chilling, the day before, with the fever that rose from the newly-broken prairie. The three of them sat quiet only a moment.

"Why does he frisk his tail so?" Davie asked.

"He's praising the Lord," replied Hughie, wise and wan.

"Is he now!" exclaimed Davie, impressed. "Does God like it?"

"Fine," said Hughie. That was an easy one. "It's in the Psalm. Creeping things and all ye cattle."

Davie sat for some time sharing his Maker's pleasure in the antics of happy calves. Then bored—perhaps like his Maker—he turned to other things. He rose, and went down the path towards the road, and stood looking down it, in the direction from which the older children must come, surely soon now, from school. Only here and there along that path where they would appear was the grass not higher than the children's heads; in some places it was higher than a man on horseback. There seemed no children in sight.

But wasn't that someone coming down there on the other road?

"I see somebody coming on the road, Hughie!" he called.

"You do not!" answered Hughie. It wasn't at all likely anybody was coming. Yet in case anything so unusual was happening, he would just have a look. Sarah waddled after him.

Ship ahoy!

Was that really something moving down there in the further slough? The three stood still, peering across the prairie, hands sheltering eyes, barefooted, the boys in the most primitive of homemade overalls, Sarah in an apron unadorned, the golden autumn sunshine blowing around them. They stood looking....

Then the home-coming children emerged from the tall grass into which the younger ones were strongly forbidden to go, because children sometimes got fatally lost in it, and at this signal the three ran to meet them, crying out the news. Gaining the little rise of ground again, upon which the house stood, they all paused together to look at whatever it was that drew near, Mary, the oldest of them, the teacher, Jessie and Flora, James and Peter.

Yes! There was no doubt about it now!

"'Tis a team!" cried Peter.

"'Tis a pair of grays!" he added in a moment. They were all perfectly motionless from curiosity now. Who had grays in that neighborhood?

"There's two men in it," Mary affirms.

Then Peter yells,

"One is wearing blue!" They can scarcely breathe now.

Blue! Can it be blue! This is too much for Mary.

"Run, Peter!" she cries. "Tell mother! Get father! It has the looks of a soldier!" It is three weeks now since the last battle, since word has come from Wully. The little girls are jumping about in excitement.

The children's shouts had not at all disturbed the mother in the kitchen, where she sat sewing, until—could she believe her ears?—they were shouting, "'Tis Wully, mother! 'Tis Wully!" She ran out of the house, down the path.

"It never is!" she says, unsteadily. But she can see someone in blue, someone standing up, waving a cap now. She can see his white face. The children bolt down the road. She can see him, her black-bearded first-born. The driver is whipping up the horses. Home from battles, pale to the lips, he is in her arms. But she is paler.

"Run for your father!" she cries, to whoever will heed her. The children are pulling at him boisterously. The strange driver is patting his horses, his back to the family reunited. Hugged, and kissed, and patted and loved, the bearded Wully turns to the stranger.

"This is Mr. Knight, of Tyler, mother. He brought me all the way."

"'Tis a kind thing you have done!" she exclaims, shaking his hand devoutly.

"Oh, he was a soldier. And he didn't look able to walk so far."

"You're not sick!" she cries to Wully, scanning his face. Certainly he was not sick, now. He could have walked it, but he was glad he didn't have to, he adds, smiling engagingly at the stranger. They stand together awkwardly, joy-smitten, looking at one another, excited beyond words. Then the mother leads the way to the unpainted house, the children hanging to Wully, dancing about.

The fifteen-year-old Andrew was working in the farther part of the field just below the house that afternoon, when he saw, from a distance, his father, called by Peter, suddenly leave his plow, and run towards the house surely faster than an old man ever runs. His own team was fly-bitten and restless, and he left it just long enough to see that in front of the house there was a team and a light wagon. He unhitched his half-broken young steers, urged them impatiently to the nearest tying place, and hurried to the house.

What he saw there made so great an impression on him, that fifty-seven years later, when that stranger's grandson was one of the disheartened veterans of the World War who came to his office looking for work, the whole scene rose before him in such poignancy that he had to turn his head away abruptly, remembering....

There in the kitchen, in his mother's chair sat the stranger in the fine clothes, with a drink of whisky in his hand which his father had just poured out. There on the bed sat his great gaunt brother in blue, one

The Able McLaughlins by Margaret Wilson

Margaret Wilhelmina Wilson was born on the 16th January 1882 in Traer, Iowa.

Her early years were spent on the family farm before she enrolled at the University of Chicago and obtained degrees in 1903 & 1904.

On graduating she became a missionary for the United Presbyterian Church of North America and was sent to the Punjab in India to work at a girl's school and then a hospital.

Illness meant a return home in 1910. She would spend the next few years at the divinity school of The University of Chicago and to teach at West Pullman High School. She also took care of her invalided father and wrote a number of short stories which were published in various magazines including the Atlantic Monthly. Many of these explored the role of religion and the secondary status of women in society.

In 1923 she won a $2000 writing prize offered by Harper & Brothers. That same year she married George Douglas Turner, who she had met in India 19 years before.

Turner was a tutor at Brasenose College, Oxford and later the warden of Dartmoor Prison. She was now to live in England.

In 1924 she was awarded the Pulitzer Prize for her novel 'The Able McLaughlins'

She continued to write, using in various novels, her experiences of all those years before in India and to continue to explore women's role in society although, at times, her critics were apt to label her work as melodramatic.

Her interest in penal reform provoked a non-fiction study 'The Crime of Punishment' (1931) and also influenced two of her eight adult novels, 'The Dark Duty' (1931) and 'The Valiant Wife' (1933). Her final work was a children's book 'The Devon Treasure Mystery' (1939).

Margaret Wilhelmina Wilson died on the 6th October 6, 1973.

Index of Contents

THE ABLE McLAUGHLINS

CHAPTER I

The prairie lay that afternoon as it had lain for centuries of September afternoons, vast as an ocean; motionless as an ocean coaxed into very little ripples by languid breezes; silent as an ocean where only very little waves slip back into their element. One might have walked for hours without hearing anything louder than high white clouds casting shadows over the distances, or the tall slough grass bending lazily into waves. One might have gone on startled only by the falling of scarlet swamp-lily seeds, by sudden goldfinches, or the scratching of young prairie chickens in the shorter grasses. For years now not even a baby buffalo had called to its mother in those stretches, or an old squaw broken ripening wild grapes from the creek thicket. Fifteen years ago one might have gone west for months without hearing a human voice. Even that day a traveler might easily have missed the house where little David and the fatter little Sarah sat playing, for it was less in the vastnesses about it than one short bubble in a wave's crest. Ten years ago the children's father had halted his ox team there, finishing his journey from Ayrshire, and his eight boys and girls alighting upon the summer's crop of wild strawberries, had harvested it with shrieks of delight which broke forever the immediate part of the centuries' silence. A solitary man would have left the last source of human noise sixty miles behind him, where the railroad ended. But this farsighted pioneer had brought with him a strong defense against the hush that maddens. He had a real house now. The log cabin in which he and his nine, his brother and his ten, his two sisters and their sixteen had all lived that first summer, was now but a mere woodshed adjoining the kitchen. The house was a fine affair, built from lumber hauled but forty miles—so steadily the railroad crept westward—and finished, the one half in wild cherry cut from the creek, and the other half in walnut from the same one source of wood. Since the day of the first McLaughlin alighting there had arrived, altogether, to settle more or less near him, on land bought from the government, his three brothers and four sisters, his wife's two brothers and one sister, bringing with them the promising sum of sixty-nine children, all valiant enemies of quietness and the fleeing rattlesnakes. Some of the little homes they had built for themselves could be seen that afternoon, like distant specks on the ocean. But Sarah and David had no eyes just then for distant specks.

They had grown tired of watching the red calf sleep, and Davie was trying to make it get up. Finally in self-defense, it rose, and having found itself refreshed, began gamboling about, trying its length of rope, trouser leg rolled up to his hairy knee. There on a strip of carpet in front of the bed knelt his mother with a strange white face, soaking bloody rags away from evil-looking sores on that precious foot. There by the cupboard stood Mary, tearing something white into bandages, with the children huddled around her, awed by the sight of their mother.

Andy saw all that the moment that Wully, taking up one of the children's old jokes, cried out to him, in a voice that belied his foot, a greeting that the young ones had loved deriding.

"Lang may your lum reek, Andy!" There wasn't really anything wrong with Wully, it seemed. That wasn't a wound, he affirmed. It was only a scratch. He really couldn't say just how it had happened. It wasn't anything! It might not be anything to a soldier, but to his mother it was the mark of imminent death for her dearest son. She began rubbing it gently with lambs' fat. Wully, bethinking himself, pulled from a pocket a paper-wrapped bundle of sweeties for the children, who saw such things but seldom. They were intent upon the contents of that, and the stranger was talking to his father, when Andy, still standing awkwardly in the door, saw a thing happen which was a landmark in his understanding. He saw his mother, who had made fast the last bandage, and was carefully pulling down the trouser leg, suddenly bend over and kiss that leg! Such passion he saw in that gesture that he realized vaguely then some great fierce hidden thing in life, escaping secrecy only at times, a terrible thing called love ... which breaks forth upon occasions ... even in old women like his mother. He turned his face away suddenly as from some forbidden nakedness, and fixed his eyes upon Wully.

That hero, quite unabashed, was pulling his mother, who had risen, down to a seat beside him on the bed. She sat there, unconscious of the roomful, just looking at him, looking ... as if she could never see his face enough. She watched him devouringly when presently, with the attention of them all, he began light-heartedly telling about his escape. Half of his regiment had been made prisoners, including his major. They had been marched away towards a train, to be sent south, and he had marched among them until he dropped. He told his captors that they could shoot him if they would, but he couldn't go a step further. They had left him lying helpless there by the roadside, a guard standing over him. And before the wagon came along, which was to pick them up, the guard had slept, and Wully, stronger to run to freedom than to march to prison, had made his escape. Starved and hiding, he had crept night by night towards the Mississippi, and there he had seen a boat which was bringing Northern wounded men home, tie up at the river bank to bury its dead. Its captain had taken pity on him, chilling and nauseated, and had brought him to Davenport. Then when he had got by train to the nearest Iowa town, this stranger had shown him this kindness.... Oh, his mother needn't worry about his being shot for a deserter. They knew him too well in his company, if there was any of them left. And hadn't his chum, Harvey Stow, been home four times to visit, without permission from anyone, and had he ever been punished for it? As soon as he had something to eat, and he could find where to report, he would be going back—yes, certainly—going back, however much his mother caught her breath at the mention of it.

It was so interesting to hear him talk that the men could scarcely leave for their duties. But there were the horses to feed, and the cows to milk, and the kind strange team to reward. Mr. Knight followed the boys to the barn and watched with amusement how reverently they rubbed down and bedded and fed the guests of the stable. And when they came in again, there sat the scrubbed soldier, in a fresh hickory shirt and clean jeans, in his mother's chair, his swathed foot on a stool—the stool was Hughie's thought—and the New York Tribune in his hand—the paper was Flora's contribution. He was talking grinningly to his mother. A white cloth was spread on the table, and the mother, shining, uplifted with joy, was wiping pink-banded cups which Wully remembered to have seen taken from the sacred shelf only when her Scot cousin, who had come to this country to enlighten the darkness of the Yankees by taking the presidency of one of their colleges, had come west to visit this family. Not since then had the Scottish sheets been out of the chest, and now they were airing on the line. 'Twas an occasion magnificent to consider! When they sat down at the table for supper—and they had not long to wait, for the mother was that woman of whom tradition says she could make a pair of jean pants in twenty minutes—they had fried prairie chicken, and potatoes and scons and egg-butter, and stewed wild plums, sweetened with sugar at forty cents a pound. The father instituted the feast by a long prayer. "Of course!" thought the stranger. "They're Scotch!" He counted the children. There were ten.

"You've a fine family," he commented.

"Not so bad when they're all here," returned the mother complacently. "There's a boy and a girl away at school." She paused abruptly.

"Our boy younger than Wully was killed at Fort Donaldson," explained the father.

"Ah! My son was wounded there. Lost a hand." There was a moment's silence. Then Wully said, wanting the subject changed,

"It's over now, mother. Grant'll get them now."

They proceeded to talk of the coming election. Five families of Covenanting Scotch in the neighborhood were deserting the principles of their forefathers and taking out naturalization papers, hoping to vote for Lincoln. The visitor wondered vaguely what kind of Scotch that might be. He had no chance to ask. The mother seemed to have read every word of the last Tribune. He had hardly time for that himself. She seemed a woman of wide information. Apparently she knew the position of every unit of the army.

Supper was over. Flora handed her father The Book, and moved the candle near him. He found the place, and said,

"The twenty-third Psalm."

To the man's surprise, the mother began the song in a clear, sure voice, and the children all joined, without hesitation, as if this was a part of a familiar routine. The boys and girls were obviously thinking of the guests of honor. The mother's face was turned to her son. But the father was looking away in a dream to something he seemed to see through the wall before him. When the singing was over, he began reading from The Book words that clearly had some exalted meaning to him, though what it might be the stranger could not imagine. "Lift up your heads, O ye gates, and be ye lift up, ye everlasting doors, and the King of glory shall come in. Who is this King of glory? The Lord strong and mighty, the Lord mighty in battle." It sounded impressive, read with a subdued ring in the voice. Then he shut the book, in a high silence, and they all moved their chairs back, and knelt down. The stranger knelt, too, somewhat tardily. Not that he objected to prayers, of course. He was a religious man himself in a way. His wife often went to church. He could see the rapt face of the father praying in great, sonorous phrases which sounded vaguely familiar. Of all the children he could see, not one had an eye open. They were thanking the Lord for the boy's return. "Bless the Lord, oh my soul, and all that is within me, bless His holy name." They proceeded to pray for everyone in the United States, the President and his cabinet, the generals and the colonels and the captains, all the privates, all the sick and homesick, for those destroyed by war, for the mourning and all small children, for slaves in their freedom, and masters in their poverty, and then for the stranger, that he might hear the Judge say unto him, "Come, ye blessed of my Father, inherit the kingdom prepared for you from the beginning of the world. For I was sick, and ye ministered unto me"; "that the beauty of the Lord, as now, might be upon him forever." The stranger had scarcely got over that when they all began saying the Lord's Prayer together. "Nothing lacking but the collection," he thought, somewhat resentfully. Not having heard a sermon for some time, he had forgotten that. When they rose from their knees, Sarah and David were found asleep. Andy picked them up and carried them away to bed. And even while Mr. Knight was wondering how many of the children he would have to sleep with, the mother took the sheets from beside the stove, and as she started for the fine parlor, whose bed was to be got ready for the guest, she said,

"Wully is to have the kitchen bed by himself. You all just go upstairs and leave him alone."

The stranger had the decency to go soon to his bed. It wasn't a half-bad bed, either. And he was tired. It had been a sudden impulse, this driving the soldier home, with a new team, over no road at all. But he was glad he had come. He had wanted to see this country. The new horses had jogged along very well. Moreover, he had made friends among the Scotch, and he was a politician. He thought of his son with Sherman's army. He thought of the soldier's impressive mother. He smiled over the number of children. He slept.

But long after the house was quiet, Wully lay talking to his father and mother, who sat on his kitchen bed. He told them of marches and battles and fevers and skirmishes, none of which had endangered him at all, of course, of the comradeship among the boys from the Yankee settlement down the creek, and of the hope everywhere, now, that the end was near. Then gradually there fell a silence over them, an understanding silence, wherein each knew the other's thoughts. They were all thinking of that first terrible home-coming of his, of the things that led up to it. He remembered how "the boys" had been eating breakfast in camp, when the orders came that meant their first battle. He had been in an agony of fear lest he might be afraid. The one good thing about it was that Allen, his brother, had been sent away on a detail not an hour before. He would go into battle without having his brother to worry about. That trembling, as he advanced, had not been fear, but only ague so severe he might have stayed behind if he had chosen. But he had advanced with the rest of them, and in the darkness when he tried to sleep after it was over, he knew he need not fear cowardice again. They had won the day, and they exulted as fiercely as they had fought. Had not their regiment been one of three which, not getting their orders to retreat, had stood firmly till fresh troops came to save the day! But the next morning's task had mocked terrifyingly their victory. He could have pleaded fever to escape from that.... Some on the snow-covered hillside were digging great trenches, some were throwing body after body into them, some were shoveling earth in upon them. He had bent down to tug at a stiff thing half hidden by snow, he had turned it over, a head grotesquely twisted backward, a neck mud-plastered, horrible, bloody. Then he had cried out, and fallen down. That thing, with the lower face shot away, was Allen! His comrades, hunting about, found the bodies of the others of the little squad that had been hurriedly recalled.

That night Wully had planned to desert. He had announced his intention to his lieutenant who came to sit beside him. They might drum him out of camp as a deserter if they would. He was telling them plainly what he intended doing. He would never fight again. But before he was able to walk, his comrades had got him a furlough. They understood only too well his fever and his delirium, and they remembered how he had gone through the battle, vomiting and ague-shaken, firing with a hand too weak to aim, and vomiting again, and shaking and firing. All the way home he had planned how to break the news to his mother. But when he had seen her, his grief which before had had no outlet, suddenly burst forth, so that even as she asked him, he was sobbing it all out to her. He had never told her, of course, how

Allen's sweet singing mouth had been destroyed. For Allen had been a gay lad, playing the fiddle, and singing many songs, sometimes little lovable ones he made as he sang, about pumpkins, or the old red rooster, or anything that might please the little children.

For Wully, no home-coming could ever again be so terrible as that one. But his father and mother who sat beside him there were trying not to know that just such news might come at any time of this one, who must go back to death's place. Wully lay telling them little things he could recall of those last days. Had he told them of the time that the captain had stood, unbeknown to Allen, behind a bush, listening to him imitate all the company's officers? There had never been a day that Allen had not been called upon to make fun for his comrades. Laughter had bubbled up within him and gushed out even in stark times. There was no detail of his nonsense not precious to the two who listened. It was late before they left him, and he soon slept. Towards morning, his mother slept.

Soon after daylight the stranger came into the kitchen. The mother was standing half hidden by the steam that rose from the milk pails that she was scalding out. The oldest sister at a table where candlelight and dawn struggled together, was packing a school lunch into a basket. A small girl was buttoning fat Sarah into her dress. Two small boys were struggling with their shoes on the floor. Wully presently hobbled in from out of doors, declaring himself recovered, a giant refreshed. The stranger noticed that when they found their places at the table, there was a larger child beside each smaller one, to look after him. There was one little fellow who looked like the soldier, and a half-grown sister with beautiful regular features like his. But the others were all alike, with deeply set dark blue eyes, long upper lips, and lower faces heavy, keen, determined. He could have appreciated what the mother said sometimes simply, to the neighbors, when they remarked how good her children were: "Yes, they're never any care when they're well. If we had one or two, we might let them have tantrums. But who could live in a house with thirteen ill bairns?" Since by that she meant, of course, naughty children, her question seemed indeed unanswerable.

Now they sat eating lustily their cornmeal, and she talked with leisure and understanding. When the meal was finished, Flora handed her father The Book again.

"By Golly!" said the stranger to himself, "they're going to do it again!" And they did. The mother lifted the Psalm from memory, and then they repeated some part of the Bible. The stranger was the more ill at ease because young Hughie's eyes were fixed accusingly upon him. Again the father prayed for all the inhabitants of the world, by name or class.

When the boys brought the guest's wonderful team to the door, all the family gathered to bid him good-by.

"I wish you well, sir, for your kindness," the father said, and the mother, at a loss to know how to thank him sufficiently, added,

"We'll never forget this, neither us nor our children!" It was that trembling choked back in her voice that gave the stranger's grandson his work with the firm of Andrew McLaughlin, in the fall of 1920.

The beautiful grays started impatiently away, the men went to their work, and the children to their school. In the kitchen his mother bandaged Wully's feet, and put the wee'uns out of door to play while he had a sleep. At half past eleven he woke. His mother was sitting in the doorway, shelling beans. How was he to guess that she was late with her dinner preparations because again and again she had to stop, and look at this child of hers grown a strange man in the midst of horrors unimaginable? He lay very still looking at her. The kettle was singing on the stove. Through the door, he saw the red calf sleeping in the sunshine. A wave of joy, of ecstasy complete passed over him. Oh, the heaven of home, the peace of it, of a good bed, of a mother calmly getting dinner!

"I'm starved, mother!" he sang out suddenly to her. She hurried to the cellar, and brought him cool milk and two cookies. The children, hearing him, came in to watch him. He sat down in the doorway, and began throwing beans up, and catching them skillfully, to win the friendship of the doubtful little Sarah. David watched him eagerly. Presently Hughie said:

"Mother, why did yon strange man not say the Psalm?"

"You mus'na stare so at visitors, Hughie!"

"But why, mother? Why did he not say it?"

"Maybe he did'na ken it."

"Did'na ken what?"

"The Psalm."

"Did'na ken the fifteenth Psalm, and him a man grown!" Hughie had never seen anyone before who couldn't say the fifteenth Psalm.

"Aw, mother!" he exclaimed remonstratingly. "Even Davie knows that!"

Wully chuckled. He knew the world. He had seen cities. He had marched across states. He had eaten ice cream.

CHAPTER II

Wully slept the whole afternoon, and that evening the aunts and uncles and cousins began coming to see him. He and Allen, being among the oldest of the clan's young fry, had been the first to enlist, though since then two of the McNairs, a Stevenson, and a McElhiney had grown old enough to fight. Allen's death and Wully's spectacular career had endeared him to the neighbors. They had suffered with him, they thought. Two years before, when they had gathered to offer their consolation to the family because he was reported dead, they had found his mother rejecting sympathy with as much decision as was civil. The United States government might be a powerful organization, but it could never make her believe that Wully had been shot in the back, running away from duty. The Stowes doubtless did well to array themselves in mourning for Harvey, but she knew her son was alive. And sure enough, after three weeks a letter came, no larger than the palm of her hand. She knew it had come when she saw a nephew running towards the house to give it to her. On one side, the little paper had said that Wully was alive and well in a prison in Texas, and on the other, crowded together, were ten names of comrades imprisoned with him, and Harvey Stowe's name was written first and largest. That minute she had buttoned the bit of paper into Andy's shirt pocket, and sent him fifteen miles down the creek to tell the Stowes to take off their mourning, and the clan, hearing the news from the mad-riding Andy had gathered to rejoice with her. And now that the exciting Wully was home again, they brought him wild turkeys, and the choice of the wild plums, an apple or two, first fruit of their new orchards, and whatever else their poverty afforded. Mrs. Stowe came to see him, bringing a package of sugar. But the Stowes were well-to-do. The others were exclusively what Allen had dubbed "the ragged lairds of the Waupsipinnikon."

Not that their creek was really the Waupsipinnikon. Allen had only crossed that chuckling stream on his first journey with his father, but he had delighted in a name so whimsical, so rollicking, and had used it largely. Pigs and chickens of his christening bore it unharmed. And he put it into the song he used to sing sometimes, when the prairie's youth and beauty were tired of dancing to his fiddle. All the neighbors were mentioned in it:

The McWhees, the McNabs, the McNorkels,
The Gillicuddies, the McElhineys, the McDowells,
The Whannels, the McTaggerts, the Strutheres,
The Stevensons, the McLaughlins, and the Sprouls.

In his pronunciation the meter was perfect, and Sprouls and McDowells rhymed perfectly, both of them, with "holes." For an encore he would show his appreciative audience how the head of each family mentioned "asked the blessing," always politely and stubbornly refusing to imitate the master of the house in which the fun was going on—at least until the master had retired.

Between the visits of the ragged lairds and their offspring, Wully got so much sleep that on the fourth day he announced himself able to help with the fall plowing. His mother refused to have such a suggestion considered, and they compromised on his digging carrots in the garden. At that task she found him doggedly working away after an hour, white and trembling. For a week he recovered from the fever that came on, sleeping by day and by night. The twelfth day he was so well that he rode to look over the "eighty" his father had bought for him with the two hundred dollars that had accrued to him during the fourteen months he lay in prison, trying to carve enough wooden combs to earn what would keep him from starving. His father explained that he might have brought land further on at a dollar and a half an acre. But this was the choice bit of land, and, moreover, it joined the home farm. And this bit of ground, rising just here was obviously the place for the house to be built. Wully smiled indulgently at the idea of his building a house. But he wasn't to smile about it, his father protested. Indeed, they would some way get an acre broken this fall yet in time to plant maple seed, and poplar, for the first windbreak, so that the little trees would be ready for their duty.

The elder McLaughlin sighed with satisfaction as he talked. Even yet he had scarcely recovered from that shock of incredulous delight at his first glimpse of the incredible prairies; acres from which no frontiersman need ever cut a tree; acres in which a man might plow a furrow of rich black earth a mile long without striking a stump or a stone; a state how much larger than all of Scotland in which there was no record of a battle ever having been fought—what a home for a man who in his childhood had walked to school down a path between the graves of his martyred ancestors—whose fathers had farmed a rented sandpile enriched by the blood of battle among the rock of the Bay of Luce. Even yet he could scarcely believe that there existed such an expanse of eager virgin soil waiting for whoever would husband it. Ten years of storm-bound winters, and fever-shaken, marketless summers before the war, had not chilled his passion for it—nor poverty so great that sometimes it took the combined efforts of the clan to buy a twenty-five cent stamp to write to Scotland of the measureless wealth upon which they had fallen. From the time he was ten years old, he had dreamed of America. He had had to wait to realize his dream till his landlord had sold him out for rent overdue. What Wully remembered gallingly about that sale was that his grandmother had been present at it, and her neighbors, thinking she bought the poor household stuff to give back to her son, refused to bid for it against her. Then, having got it all cheap, she sold it at considerable profit, and pocketed the money. That was why, taught by his father, he despised everything that suggested Scottish stinginess. Nor had he wept a tear when the old woman died, soon after, and his father, taking his share of her hoardings, had departed for his Utopia. Some of the immigrants had long since lost their illusions. But not John McLaughlin. He loved his land like a blind and passionate lover. Really there was nothing glorious that one was not justified in imagining about a nation to be born to such an inheritance. And he told Wully that he might at least console himself with the thought that those months in prison had made him possessor of such land, that with the possible exception of the fabled Nile valley, there was probably in the world no richer. And the McLaughlins prided themselves on the fact that they were no American "soil-scratchers," exhausting debauchers of virgin possibilities. Their rich soil, they promised themselves, was to be richer by far for every crop it yielded.

The next day Wully felt so well that he must have something to do. On the morrow the bi-weekly mail would be in, and if it brought orders for him, he would be returning to his regiment. He stood in the doorway looking toward his father's very young orchard, and considering the possibilities of the afternoon. Of course, he might ride over and see Stowe's sweetheart, who had come to see him the other time he was home ill. But he dreaded talking to a strange woman. She was pretty, certainly. That was why he was afraid of her. If he had been Allen, now, with an excuse for going to see a pretty girl, his horse would have been in a lather before he arrived. Wully had envied Stowe, sometimes, his eagerness for just a certain letter. It must, he thought in certain moods, after all be rather pleasant to have someone so dear that a man like Stowe would endanger his honor, and life itself by stealing away to see her. Stowe was to be married as soon as he got home. He was so close a friend that he talked to Wully about that. If Stowe had had a site for a house waiting him, as Wully had, he would have talked his friend deaf. But just the same, Wully wasn't going to see his sweetheart. He would do anything for Stowe but that. Easing his conscience by that assurance, he heard his mother speaking to him.

If he wanted something to do, would he ride over to Jeannie McNair's for her? She wanted to know if Jeannie had any news yet from Alex. When would that man be back, she wondered indignantly. Who ever heard of a man harvesting a wheat crop, and starting back to Scotland, leaving his family alone with the snakes—she always added the snakes because the McNair cabin was on low land which those reptiles rather affected—and all to prevent his half brothers from getting a bit more of a poor inheritance than they were entitled to! If Wully went on her errand, he was to take poor Jeannie a few prairie chickens, and those three young ducks she had raised for her, alone there with her bairns!

And if he was going, he must put on his uniform. He demurred. She insisted. Why, Jeannie had never seen him in his uniform! He smiled to hear her imply that not to have seen him so arrayed was the greatest of her deplorable privations. Yet he went and put it on, nevertheless, for it was the most handsome suit he had ever had, always before having been clothed in the handiwork of his mother and sisters. When he was ready to go, the ducks caught and tied, a bit of jelly safely wrapped, as he stood by the horse, in his mother's sight the most beautiful soldier in the American armies, she said:

"Jeannie's Jimmie was just your age, you mind, Wully."

She watched him riding away, the fondness of her face ministering to the joyous sense of well-being that swept over him. How unspeakably lovely the country was! How magnificent its richness! He had never felt it so keenly before. He must be getting like his father. Or perhaps it looked so much more impressive because he had seen so much swampy desolation in the South. The grass he rode through seemed to bend under the sparkling of the golden sunshine. He came to the creek, and as he crossed it he remembered with a pang the time his companions had staggered thankfully and hastily to drink out of a pool covered with green slime. He turned with disgust from the memory. He wouldn't even think of those things to spoil his few days at home. He gave himself up to the persuasive peace around him. He rode along, completely, unreasonably happy. He began to sing. Singing, he remembered Allen. How was it that he was here singing, and Allen, the singer, was dead! But the afternoon's glow took away soon even the bitterness of that question.

He came presently in sight of the McNairs' cabin. Though every other man of the neighborhood had been able, thanks to the wartime price of wheat, to build for his family a more decent shelter than the first one, that Alex McNair, fairly crazy with land-hunger, added acre to acre, regardless of his family's needs. Such a man Wully scorned with all the arrogance of youth. He had, moreover, understood and shared something of his mother's pity for her beloved friend, McNair's wife. He remembered distinctly that when his parents had been leaving the Ayrshire home for America, Jeannie had put into his hand a poke of sweeties to be divided by him among the other children during the journey. That had been a happy farewell, because Jeannie and her five were soon to follow. But when the ten flourishing McLaughlins again saw Jeannie on this side of the water, of her five there remained only her little Chirstie, and a baby boy. The bodies of the other three she had seen thrown out of the smallpox-smitten ship which the feasting sharks were following. Since then she had been a silent woman, though Wully's mother spoke of her sometimes, sighing, as a girl of high spirits and wit. Now, however much other Ayrshire women might rejoice in a dawning nation, the memory of those bloody mouths stood always between her and hope. She endured the new solitude without comment or complaint. Homesick for a hint of old-country decency, she hung the walls of her cabin with the linen sheets of her dowry, sheets that must have come out of the poisonous ship. Wully's mother admired that immaculate room without one sigh of envy. White sheets would keep clean a long time in that cabin, with only the two bairns. But she thanked God that in her crowded cabin there was not room for one sheet on the wall. Moreover, in the new land, Jeannie had lost two babies, so that now for her labor and travail, she had only the Scottish two, and a baby girl. With another baby imminent, her husband had "trapassed" away to Scotland! He was too "close" to have taken her with him. But not for the wealth of Iowa would she have exposed her children again to sea. She would stay and save them on dry land. She wouldn't be left altogether alone. Her brother's family lived but two miles away.

Wully rode up to the house unperceived, though not one tree, not one kindly bush protected it against the immensity of the solitude around it. He tied his horse, and was at the door before Jeannie saw him. Then she exclaimed:

"If it is'na Isobel's Wully!" She shook his hand, and patted him on his shoulder, and reached up and kissed him. He didn't mind that. She was practically an aunt, so intimate were the families. In her silent excitement she brought him into her wretched little cabin.

And there stood another woman. By the window—a young woman—turning towards him with sunshine on her white arms—and on the dough she was kneading—sunshine on her white throat—and on the little waves of brown hair about her face—sunshine making her fingertips transparent pink—a woman like a strong angel—beautiful in light!

Wully just stared.

"It's only Chirstie." Jeannie was surprised at his surprise.

Only Chirstie!

"She was just a wee'un when I saw her," he stammered. "I did'na ken she was so bonny!" Fool that he was! Idiot! Yammering away in bits of a forsaken dialect! What would the girl think of him!

"It's more than four years you've been away," Jeannie reminded him kindly. She began plying him with questions. He answered them realizing that the girl was covering her bread with a white cloth freshly shaken from its folds—that she was washing her hands, and pulling down her sleeves—and seating herself near him composedly enough. His mother was well, he said. They were all well. It was twelve days now since he had come home. Yes, he was tired of the war. The more he saw of the girl, the tireder he got. The other boys from the neighborhood were all alive and well as far as he knew. He looked at that girl as much as he dared. He could think of nothing to say—that is, of nothing he dared yet to say. He was most stupidly embarrassed, trying not to appear foolish. He stammered out that his mother had sent over some things, some squashes—he would go and bring them in. He went out to get them. Oh, it wasn't squashes! It was ducks! The girl giggled deliciously. Her mother smiled. Wully was more at his ease. Now where should they put the ducks? They were all standing together now in the dooryard, the three ducks, the three humans. There was no place ready for the gifts. Well, Wully would make a coop for them. Just give him a few sticks. But there were no sticks. Then Chirstie thought of some bits of wood behind the barn. They went and got them. She stood, shy because of the ardor of his eyes, by her mother, watching his skill in making duck shelters. He could have gone on making them forever. But the work was done. He grew embarrassed again.

He must be going. Not before he had had tea! He didn't really care for tea. He would have—just a drink of water. No sooner had he said that word than he regretted it painfully. There was no fresh water. But Chirstie would go get some. He knew that one of the things that annoyed his mother most about the McNair place was that Alex had never even dug a second well. The water was all still carried a quarter of a mile from the old well in the slough. Chirstie was ready to start for his drink at once. Was he not a soldier, and a fine looking one, her eyes inquired demurely, whom she would be honored to serve? No, he would get it himself.

"Go along, the two of you!" said Jeannie. And as they started, she stood in the door looking after them, and on her face there grew a sore and tender smile.

He took the pail. She reached for the big stick. That was to kill rattlesnakes. He took that, too, shocked by the thought of death near her feet. They walked silently together, in a path just wide enough for one. Their hands touched at times. He grew bold to turn and study her beauty. Their eyes met, but she said never a word. On they went, silently. He could hear his heart beating presently. He forgot that his feet had ever been sore. He could have walked on that way with her to Ayrshire. They came to the well. His hand trembled as he let the pail down into it. That may have been the ague. He filled the cup, and gave it to her to drink, looking straight at her. She put it to her lovely lips and drank, looking across the prairie. She handed it back to him, and he took it, and her hand. The grass about the well was very high. Some way—he put out his arms, and she was in them.

"Chirstie!" he whispered. "I didn't know that you were here! I didn't know that you were the lassie for me!" He kissed her fearfully. He kissed her without fear, many times. She said only "Oh!" He held her close.

After a time—how long a time it must have been to have worked so mightily!—she sighed and said:

"We must go back."

Hand in hand they went back, until they came to the edge of the tall grass. They couldn't miss the last of that opportunity. Out in the short grass she pulled her hand away. No one must see yet, she said. Of course not. Not yet.

No, he said to Jeannie, he couldn't stay for tea. He had had his drink. He had indeed drunk deep.

He rode out into the loveliness of the distances, unconscious of everything but that girl in the sunlight. He was shaken through with the excitement of her lips. Her name sang itself riotously through his brain. Perhaps in a thousand miles there was not a man so surprised as that one. But he was not thinking of his emotions. He was thinking of what he had found. He was looking through vistas opened suddenly into the meaning of life. He was seeing glimpses of its space and graciousness. He laughed aloud abruptly remembering the site his father had chosen for his house. And yesterday a house had meant nothing to him! He was getting too near home. He had come to the creek. He stopped his horse, and sat still, going over again and again that supreme moment. He had never kissed a girl before in his life. Allen had kissed them whenever he had gotten a good chance—or any chance at all. Now, to-day, with Chirstie, it had been just simply the only thing to do. She was already by the significance of that caress a part of him. Oh, no wonder Stowe had come home four times! And now his holiday was all but over. He vowed rashly he would not go back! Never! If only he had come and found her the first of his twelve days! He wondered why he had left her. He might have stayed for supper. But no, not with her mother there! He was glad he had come away. To think of him, who had marched through states and territories, finding a girl like that, the very queen of beauty, right there on the prairie! He could scarcely remember how she had looked when he had seen her last. Just some kind of a little girl—no stunning queen like this. The song of her name rose and fell in his mind rhythmically. The sun grew low while he sat exulting. A chill came into the air. He couldn't endure to take his excitement home to the light. He would wait till they would all be at supper. How glad his mother would be when sometime she heard of his love! He knew it was the very thing she would have chosen for him.

When he came into the kitchen she said, with relief:

"You're a long time away, Wully!"

He replied without a waver:

"I stopped for a swim in the creek."

She sat looking at him, wondering why he was pale again, and silent. He was far from well, she was thinking. And before the meal was over, he was wondering why the children's chatter was so strangely tiresome. Wouldn't they ever get away to bed, and leave him to his memories? Even with that babbling about, he could feel her face against his....

His Uncle Peter's Davie came in with the mail after supper, bringing a paper with a notice for the scattered men of his regiment, and paroled prisoners. They were to have reported yesterday to headquarters. He tried to appear eager to go. His mother lifted the Psalm, when the visitors were gone, and left the children to quaver through it. And when he was lying in his bed, vowing desperately he would not go back, she came to him.

"I canna' thole your going, Wully!" she cried to him, and her cry braced him. He remembered with shame how she had made him go back after Allen's death, how she had signaled fiercely to him to keep the mention of anything else from the children. As if he, her son, could not do whatever he must do, and do it well! She had been ashamed of him before the children, then. He remembered that, and grew brave now. He hated to remember what a baby he had been. As if, however terrible the war might be, it hadn't to be fought out, some way, by men! As if he must escape from the hell other men must endure! He was glad now he had occasion to strengthen the strengthener.

"It's almost over now, mother!" he kept saying. Almost over, indeed, and a bullet the death of a second! What was the use of saying that when an hour could kill thousands? She sat stroking his hair, her face turned away from him, so that he suspected tears. She felt like an old broken woman, worn out not by years and childbearing, but by this war. All that night she lay sleepless, praying for her son. He lay sleepless in the room next to her, never giving her a thought. He gave all his thoughts, he gave all he had, to the girl of the slough well.

The dream of the night wore away, and the nightmare of the morning was upon him. His father was calling him long before daybreak. He was starting away, in the darkness, in the cold, away from Chirstie, towards his duty. His feet ached. His back ached. His head ached. His heart ached. He was one new great pain. It didn't seem possible that life could be so hard. But on his father drove, through the first shivering glimpses of dawn, towards the train.

CHAPTER III

After more than three months spent in hospitals, Wully came home the next March, honorably discharged from the army. His father met him at the end of the railroad, and before dawn they started westward over the all but impassable paths called roads. Rain began falling when the sun should have begun shining. Hour after slow hour of the morning their horses strained and plunged and splashed through deep, black mud. At every slough the men alighted to pull and tug at the sunken wagon, and returned bemired to their wet blankets. From noon till dusk they rode on, pulling grain sacks helmetwise down over their caps to protect the back of their necks from trickles of water, rearranging their soaked garments, hearing, when their voices fell silent, only the splashing of the horses' feet down into the thawed mud, and the sucking of the water around hoofs reluctantly lifted to take the next step. Darkness set in early, but they made the ford while there was still a soggy twilight. More soaked, more dripping, they went on, peering into the wall of blackness which settled down in front of them. They were hungry. They were tired. They were chilled to the bone. Wully's teeth chattered in spite of all he could do to prevent them. And they were both immeasurably happy. On they went, caressing the fine joy in their hearts. The father had his son home safe from battles. The son, each shivering step, was nearing the queen of the afternoon light.

At half-past eight they drew near the welcoming lighted window towards which they had strained their eyes so eagerly. If the boy had had a lesser mother, if he had been well, he would have gone on through the four miles of pouring darkness to Chirstie. But here was shelter and rest for his feebleness, a fire, food, light, a mother, and the children, caresses sprung from the warmest places in human hearts—all things, in short, that a man needs, except one. It seemed that the very kitchen breathed in great, deep sighs of thankfulness and content, this great night of its life, the night Wully got home from the army. The younger children sat watching him till they sank down from their chairs asleep, for no one thought to send them away to bed.

He had so many things to tell them that he forgot how weary he was. Now that his danger was over, he had no need of minimizing for his mother's sake the discomforts he had been suffering. He said feelingly what he thought of a government that couldn't get letters from a soldier's home in Iowa to a military hospital in New Orleans. He shouldn't have minded the fever so much if he could have heard from home, and if he had been stronger he would likely have been more sensible about not getting letters. It seemed to him he had been confined in a madhouse devised for his torture. He would have preferred a battle months long to those endless, helpless, sick-minded days. And now he never wanted to speak of that time or hear of it again as long as he lived.

Young Peter had torn his coat half off his back at play that day, and it must be mended before school time next morning. It was a piece of patching not long or difficult, but his mother laid it down to look at her Wully—she laid it down and took it again a dozen times before it was done. She couldn't deny her eyes the sight of his white, thin, beautiful face. He ought to go to bed. She could see that. She urged him to again and again, as they sat around the stove. But he had always one more thing to tell as he started to go. He had never written in full about getting back to his regiment after his last visit home, had he? Well, when he got back, there was not an officer left whom he had known. And the one to whom he had to tell his tale of escaping from his guard—oh, he was a new man, most hated by the boys—he had put Wully and two others in prison in the loft of a barn, on bread and water. And every night the guard, who knew them, used to hand up on the end of bayonets all the food they could desire. And the officer heard of it, and was more angry. He was a man who raged. And he changed the guard, and yet the men who hated his being there, in place of the colonel they had liked, Wully's friends, managed some way to feed the prisoners, so that really in the loft they had nothing to do but to sleep well-fed, and rest. And presently the new colonel waxed more raging and swearing, and sent the three away to another place to be disciplined, sent them—guess where, of all places—to Colonel Ingersoll for punishment!

"What? Not that infidel!"

Yes, exactly, and that was just how Wully had felt about it! The prisoners made Wully their spokesman in the first hearing. Colonel Ingersoll listened to them kindly till he had finished speaking. He had a boil on the back of his neck and was not able to turn his head, and he sat there, just looking at Wully, a long time, too long, Wully began to fear. And then he said:

"I wouldn't punish you if you were my man, McLaughlin. And I don't see why I should because you aren't." And he called an orderly and told him to take the men to a mess.

"Ingersoll did that? That infidel?"

"Yes."

His mother was leaning forward, Peter's coat forgotten.

"Yon's a grand man," she cried with conviction.

"He's an infidel," her husband reminded her.

"He's a grand man for a' that!" she asserted.

"But he's an infidel!"

"He's a grand man, I'm telling you, for a' that!" After that, every time she sang the antichrist's praise to her neighbors she had the last word of characterization. (After all, her family had not been Covenanters.) Presently she laid the coat down again—the children were in bed now, and Wully, too, with only his father and mother beside him in the kitchen.

"Your father told you about Jeannie's death, Wully?" His father had told him briefly about it on the way home. He didn't say to his mother that the news had thrilled him with the certainty that now his plans could have no opposition, since Chirstie was left quite unprotected, and must be needing him. He was ashamed of the hope he had had from it, when he saw his mother's face harden with grief and resentment as she went on to relate the details of her friend's death, a death grim enough to be in keeping with Jeannie's life. For her part, she hoped to live till Alex McNair got home, till she could get one good chance to tell him what she thought of him! Oh, it had been altogether a terrible winter, almost as bad as that worst early one, just one fierce-driven blizzard after another. Jeannie had known in that darkening afternoon that it was no common illness coming over her. Chirstie, terrified by her isolation, had begged to be allowed at once to go for her aunt. But even then so thick was the storm raging that from the window she could not see the barn, and to venture out into the storm could mean only death. As the night had hurled itself upon the poor little shelter, almost hidden under drifts, and the maniac wind unchecked by a tree, unhindered by a considerable hill for a thousand miles, tore on in its deadly course, inside the cabin where the candle flickered gustily out, Jeannie had whispered to her children that she was dying. One thing they must promise her so that she might die in peace. They must not venture out for help, even in the morning, unless the storm was over. She lay then moaning inarticulately, which was frightful for the children, but not so frightful as the silence that followed, when they could in no way make her answer their cries of agony. All that night Chirstie sat watching beside her, relighting the candle, while the other children slept. In the quieted morning she had helped her brother dig an entrance to the stable, and together they had got the horse out. She had wrapped him as securely as possible, and sent him across the blinding snow to his uncle's, John Keith's. And when Aunt Libby finally got there, she found the baby playing on the floor, the dinner cooking on the stove, and Chirstie on her mother's bed unconscious.

Tears were running down Isobel McLaughlin's face as she finished. Though she never doubted that God was infinitely kind, she wondered at times why that something else, called life, or nature, should be so cruel. She wondered why it was that while with her all things prospered, with the good Jeannie nothing ever refrained from turning itself into tragedy. And besides all that, now that the spring seemed coming, that stubborn girl Chirstie, refusing longer to stay with her Aunt Libby, had suddenly taken her small brother and sister, and gone back to her empty house, and there she was, living alone, with no company but occasionally a neighboring girl, or her distressed Aunt Libby. Wully's mother had gone to her, and begged her to come and stay with her. Other faithful friends had invited her to their home, but they had begged and pleaded in vain. Chirstie would listen to no one. It was a most unfitting and dangerous thing, a young girl like that alone there. She kept saying her father would be home any day now, but Isobel McLaughlin would prophesy that he would not be back till he had a new wife to bring with him. They would all see whether she was right about that or not!

Wully, the ardent, jumped instantly to the hope that Chirstie had known he was coming, and had gone back to the cabin to be there alone to receive him. That was the explanation of her "stubbornness" and indeed it was a brave thing for a girl to do for her lover. Alone there she would be this rainy night, grieving for her mother and waiting for him! Of course she would marry him at once! He would put in a crop there for her father. Tomorrow, not later than the next day, at most, they would be married! He slept but excitedly that night....

In the morning it was still raining. Breakfast and worship over, he went to the barn, where the men were setting about those rainy-day tasks which all well-regulated farms have in waiting. In the old thatched barn, three sides of which were stacked slough grass, his father was greasing the wagon's axles; Andy was repairing the rope ox harness; Peter and Hughie were struggling to lift wee Sarah into their playhouse cave in a haystack side of the barn, and having at length all but upset the wagon on themselves, propped up as it was by only three wheels, they had to be shooed away to play on the cleaner floor of the new barn. Wully took up a hoe that needed sharpening for the weeding of the corn that was to be planted. They talked of the new machine that was being made for the corn planting. Wully answered absent-mindedly that he had seen one in Davenport once. He spoke with one eye on the hoe, and one on the heavens. After an hour's waiting, the sky still forbade a journey. But his father, presently, looking up from his work, saw him climbing on a horse, wrapping himself in bedraggled blankets as best he might, against the downpour. He naturally asked in surprise:

"Wherever are you going, Wully?"

Wully replied:

"Just down the road!"

Fancy that, now! A McLaughlin answering his father in a tone that implied that what he asked was none of his business! But it was Wully who was answering, just home after four years of absence. His father was amused. The thought came gradually into his slow mind that there would be a lassie in this. A feverish man wasn't riding out through a rain like that one without some very good reason. What lassie would it be? He must ask his wife about it.

The path which Wully took required caution, but the cause demanded speed. The way seemed to have stretched out incredibly since he had last gone over it. After riding a hundred miles or so, he got to the little shanty of a barn on the McNair place. Chirstie's twelve-year-old brother Dod was there, and Wully gave his horse to his care. That horse had to be watched carefully, Wully vowed. He had never seen such tricks as it had been doing on the way over. Dod must not take his eyes from it. Wully hurried to the house.

The door of the house opened, and—Oh, damn, and all other oaths!—Scotch and army! Chirstie's aunt stood there in it, Libby Keith. She was Wully's aunt, too, that sister of his father's who had married Jeannie McNair's brother, John Keith! This was the first time that Wully had wanted really to curse an aunt, though he liked this one but dutifully. She saw him, and her voice fell in dismay.

"Lawsie me!" she bewailed. "I thought it was my Peter!"

Bad enough to be taken for her Peter at any time! And she had to stand there stupidly a moment, to recover from the disappointment, as it were, and then looking straight at him, it was like her to ask:

"Is it you, Wully?" As if she couldn't see that it was! Standing there filling the door, hiding the room from him! "Whatever is the matter?"

Where was the girl? Was his aunt a permanent blockade? He came vigorously towards her, hurrying her slow cordiality. There she was! There was Chirstie! She had seen him. He went towards her—

And she shrank away from him!

Not only had she not an impulse of welcome, she shrank away from him! She gave him her hand because she couldn't help herself.

"Chirstie!" he faltered.

"Are you back?" she asked. She pulled her hand away in a panic. "It's a fine day," he heard her murmur.

It was the bitterest day of his life! He sat down weakly. Men stagger down helplessly that way when bullets go through them. The damnable aunt began now welcoming him fondly. He didn't know what he was answering her. It couldn't be possible, could it, that Chirstie didn't want to see him? She had taken a seat just as far away from him as the room permitted. She sat about her knitting industriously. Sometimes she raised her eyes to look into the fire, but never once did she raise them to satisfy Wully's hunger. His eagerness, her refusal, became apparent at length to even the stupid aunt. She understood that Wully had got home only the night before, and in the morning, rain and all, had ridden over to see the girl who didn't want to see him. He really was looking very ill. Well, well! Isobel McLaughlin would have been mightily "set up" by such a match. If Chirstie had not been Peter's own cousin, Libby Keith would have liked nothing better than the girl for her son. She had fancied at times her son had thought of it, too. Her sympathy was with the soldier. She rose heavily after really only a few minutes, and said:

"I doubt the setting hens have left the nests, Chirstie."

She put a shawl over her head, and went to the door, and closed it after her. Wully jumped to his feet, and went to bend down over his sweetheart.

"What's the matter, Chirstie? What's the matter? What have I done?"

She shrank back into her chair.

"You haven't forgotten! You remember that afternoon! I thought now that you are alone here, we needn't wait!"

"Sit down in your chair!" she commanded. "Don't!"

He didn't. He couldn't.

"You're in my light!"

He drew back only a little way.

"I didn't say it all, but you know! Didn't you get my letters either?"

She moved farther away from him. "Now that I think of it, I guess I did. I got one or two." She looked as if she was trying to recall something trivial!

He stood absolutely dazed, looking at her hard face. Then she said:

"It's near dinner time. You'll be going back."

"I will not!" he cried, outraged. "I came for you, Chirstie! I thought we could be married right away. That's what I meant. You knew that!" He bent over her again, and she struggled away angrily. She went to the door, and called:

"Auntie! Wully's going! Do you want to see him?"

Aunt Libby came heavily in. She urged him to stay for dinner. At least she would make him something hot. Why, he was all wet from the ride!

"Don't bother about me!" he said angrily, hardly knowing his own voice. "I just rode over to see a calf of Stevenson's. I'll be on my way!" Out of the house he rushed, leaving his aunt to meditate upon her theories.

Turning back, he saw, through tears, that the girl was looking after him. He wouldn't ride towards the Stevensons. He would ride straight home, and she would know why he had come. He was chilling severely now, from the shock of her denial, from rage and humiliation and sorrow. He hardly knew whether it was tears or rain in his face. "Fool!" he kept saying to himself. Fool that he had been! Why had he ever taken so much for granted? He had had only a little letter from her, a shy letter. But he had never doubted she wrote often to him, letters which, like his mother's, had never reached him. Of course she had never really said that she would wait for him. She had never promised. But that was what that afternoon meant to him. It must be that some other man had won her. They must all be wanting her. While he had been lying in that hospital, living only on the dreams of their lovemaking, some other man had taken his place against her face. Or could it be that the tragic death of her mother had made her cold? It was no use trying to imagine that, for what ordinary, unkissed girl of the neighborhood would not have given him a decent welcome home? A mere acquaintance would have been more glad to see him back than she had been. Glad! She had not only not been glad. She had shrunk away in fear, and dread, even disgust. If it had been but mourning for her mother, she would have come to him. If he had been disconsolate, he would have known where to go for comfort! He had simply been a fool to suppose he had won her. Still, there was that afternoon to justify his hope. Could it be possible that that had meant nothing to her? Could he believe that that had been to her an accustomed experience? If only her face had blossomed just a little for him, that was all he would have asked. He could have waited, respecting her bereavement. But that shrinking away, that fear—what could he make of that? And he had supposed, fool that he was, that she felt toward him somewhat as he had felt toward her! She wanted nothing of him but his absence. All the family would hear now of his visit from Aunt Libby. Not that he would mind that, if only she had welcomed it! The wound was sickening him.

CHAPTER IV

His mother's curiosity about the lassie disappeared at the first glimpse she got of his face. She put him to bed, with hot drinks and heated stones, with quilt after quilt wrapped about him. But still he chilled and shivered. He was so wretched that she had no heart to reprove him for that rash outing through the rain.

For a long time he remained fever-shaken and low-spirited, the last one certainly she would venture to ask about a girl. Day after day he lay contrasting in his mind those two hours with Chirstie, contrasting his dreams with the reality, while the rain continued to sweep across the prairies in gray and windy majesty. One day Andy returned dripping from the post office with the news of Lee's surrender. Wully celebrated the event with an unusually hard chill. The tidings of Lincoln's death sickened him desperately. He got to thinking he was never again to be a strong man. And he could see no reason for wanting to be.

After a few weeks the rains ceased, and the spring flooded her sunshine over the fields with high engendering ecstasy. The McLaughlins, man and boy, from dawn to darkness went over their ground, getting the prodigal soil into the best possible tilth, scattering the chosen seed by hand. Even on the holy Sabbath of the Lord, Wully's father walked contentedly through his possessions, dreaming of the coming harvest, and of the eventual great harvest of a nation. It was lambing time, and calving time, and time for little pigs and chickens. The very cocks went about crowing out their conquering energy all over the yard, till it seemed to Wully, sitting wearily on the doorstep, that he was the only thing in the world sick and useless and alone.

May passed, and June. Thoughtful men sighed when they spoke of the soldier, and hated war the more. Five years ago he had gone away a strong, high-spirited lad, and now he dragged himself brokenly around the dooryard, the wreck of a man. His mother, trying to tempt his appetite, was at her wits' end. She sometimes thought if he had been a younger boy she would have given him a thoroughly good spanking. She didn't know what to make of him. Had he not always been the happiest, most even-tempered of her flock? Had there not been times when he and Allen had made bets about which one would begin chilling first, when malaria, like everything else, had been a joke with them? She had never seen a child as unhappy, as irritable as her Wully was now. There was no way of pleasing him. All he wanted was to be left alone, to lie with his face in his arms on the bed, scarcely speaking civilly when she tried to get him to eat something. But whenever she said to herself that he ought to be spanked, at once her heart reproved her. How could she imagine all that he had been through, all the strain of those years? The poor laddie, so wretched, and his own mother having no patience with him!

In all these weeks Wully had seen the girl only a few times, and none of them an occasion much less painful than the first. Once he had been well enough to go to church. He had waited till she came out of the door, and then, before them all, he had gone over to the wagon where she was seating herself with her brother. She had drawn away from him as if he had been a rattler, he said to himself bitterly. What did she suppose he had done, anyway, that she didn't want even to look in his direction? He had gone again to her desperately one evening, determined to find out what it all meant. She had indeed been alone when he came within sight, but, seeing him, she had called sharply to Dod to come and sit beside her. As if she were afraid of him! As if he would hurt her! She was even more distant now than she had been when he was in New Orleans, when he could at least think of her with hope. Once he had driven over with his mother to see her, had ridden along in forbidding silence, wondering how much his mother knew of that first visit, dreading lest she might mention Chirstie's name significantly to him. He had not condescended to go into the house that time, but finding Dod's hoe, he had weeded their little patch of corn, weeded it fiercely and well, to let her see how he would have worked for her if only she had been willing. His mother had not said a word about the girl as they rode home together, but she sighed deeply, from time to time, so that he guessed Chirstie had not even been cordial to her.

He tried hard enough, as he grew stronger, to shake off his depression. There were plenty of girls in the world whom he might marry, weren't there? The trouble was, he hated other girls. Still, he couldn't let merely one woman make him unhappy, could he? Not much! He used to be happy all the time, before he got to thinking about her so much. He would brace up, he vowed, and forget her. But Harvey Stowe came home in July, and came at once to see him, a strong and hilarious Harvey, who wouldn't take any excuses. Wully must come over to his wedding. Wully would not. Likely he would go to another man's wedding! He would have fever that day if he hadn't had it for a week! But he went.

The day after, thinking of his friend's happiness as he walked through his father's wheat, he sat down to rest in a path which it shaded, and stretched himself out in it. There suddenly and poignantly, for the first time in his life, he envied Allen and wanted to die. He wanted to die with so keen a despair that never afterwards could he hear the cocksure rail against suicide. He hated living vehemently, and wanted to escape from it. There was no use saying one girl couldn't make him unhappy. He was meant for Chirstie, and without her life had no meaning. Some way, it had just that combination of demure eyes and white arms to stimulate his desire till it was without mercy. He could not go on without her. He wished there had been a battle that day, which he could have gone into. He would have shot himself dead with his first bullet. That was the climax of his despair, though he was far from knowing it.

The next Sunday he walked with his brothers to the church where the lairds of the Waupsipinnikon, ragged but clean, worshiped the God of their fathers. The little church they had built out of their wartime prosperity stands on a green knoll on Gib McWhee's farm. Entering it, one saw then, as one sees nowadays, a large unadorned square room, with only one beauty, and that so great that any church in the world might well envy it. Eight high, narrow windows it has, pointedly arched, of clear glass, and whatever one thinks of a style of ecclesiastical architecture which draws one's attention from the sermon to the prairies, those eight windows frame pictures of billowing, cloud-shadowed, green distances in which surely sensible eyes can never sufficiently luxuriate.

Up the scrubbed aisle, into pews varnished into yellow wave patterns, family after family filed decorously that morning, mothers and infants in arms and strong men—there were as yet no old men in that world. Wully went to the family pew. Before the war he had usually sought out a place where the overflow of big boys sat as far as possible away from the source of blessings. The McLaughlin pew held only twelve, and that uncomfortably. But there had never been more than twelve children at church together, since small Sarah had been born after her brothers had gone to war.

The congregation sang their Psalms out of books now. No more lining-out of numbers in a congregation so well-established and prosperous. The man of God read the Scriptures, and then at last came that welcomed long prayer, good for fifteen minutes at least. Wully, sitting determinedly in a certain well-considered place in the pew, bowing his head devoutly and bending just a bit to one side, could watch

Chirstie through his fingers, where she sat on the other side of the church in the pew just behind the McLaughlins. Her eyes were closed, but his did a week's duty. There was no doubt about it. She was getting thinner and thinner. It wasn't just his imagination. She was paler. She was unhappy. He had noticed that week by week. Surely she was not happy!

The minister was an indecent man, cutting that prayer short in so unceremonious a fashion. Wully wondered the elders didn't notice his carelessness. But after the sermon there would be another prayer, just a glimpse long. He had that to look forward to. He made a mental note of the text, which the children would be expected to repeat at the dinner table, and then settled down, to be disturbed no more by sermons. He had long ago acquired a certain immunity to them. A breeze cooled the warm worshiping faces, and from outside came the soothing hum of bees, and the impatient stamping of fly-bitten horses. The minister's voice was rich and low. The younger children slept first, unashamedly, against the older ones next them, and then, gradually, one God-fearing farmer and another, exhausted by the week's haying, nodded, struggled, surrendered, and slept.

Wully was wide awake, waiting for the last prayer. There was no time to be lost, when the petitions were so short. He turned his head, and there—oh, Chirstie was looking at him! With head bowed, but eyes wide open, she was looking at him! Hungrily, tenderly, pitifully, just as he wanted her to look! Their eyes met, and her face blossomed red. She turned her head hastily away. Let her turn away! Let her pray! He knew, now! That was enough! For some reason she didn't mean him to understand. But he had found out! It was all right. He could wait. He could wait any length of time, if only she would look at him again in that way! The congregation had risen, and had begun the Psalm. He would tell her, then and there, how glad he was, how he understood! He lifted up his voice and sang, sang louder than anyone else. That was what Allen used to do, when the service particularly bored him. He would sing the last Psalm louder and clearer than the whole congregation, with the face of an earnest, humble angel, while his elders admired, and his contemporaries hid their amusement as best they might. Chirstie would know Wully was sending her a joyous, patient answer. What did it matter that in going out she never once would turn towards him? Perhaps that was the way of women. They don't just tell you all that is in their hearts. It was all very well. He knew what she was thinking.

After dinner, he said he was going down to the swimming hole, where the assembly of cousins proved week by week that the heat had prevailed over the shorter catechism. But instead he rushed eagerly and cautiously over to Chirstie. He knew there might be someone with her on Sunday, and he left his horse some distance away, intending, if he saw others there, to come back and wait. There was not a sound to be heard as he crept up, though he stopped, listening. He hesitated, and drew nearer. Then he saw her. She was sitting in the little plot of shade the cabin made, on the doorstep, and her head was bowed on her arms. On a bit of rag carpet on the ground, her little sister was sleeping. Chirstie didn't hear him. He went cautiously nearer, not wanting to startle her. He stood still, scarcely knowing how to be the least unwelcome. What was this he saw? What was this? She was crying! He stood still, watching her carefully. She was shaken with sobbing.

CHAPTER V

His impulse was to run and take her in his arms, but he knew now that he must be careful. You can't be impetuous, it seems, with women, at least not with that one. He had tried that once, and learned his lesson. He slipped behind the barn, and stood wondering what to do. After a few seconds he peered around cautiously. There she sat, crying shakenly. He tried vainly to imagine a reason. Perhaps her uncle was complaining of having the responsibility of her and the children alone there. Perhaps she was actually in want, perhaps in want of food. Perhaps the other girls had been talking about going away to school, and she was heartbroken because her mother's plans for her education were not to be carried out. Maybe she had just seen a snake. He remembered his mother saying that after Jeannie McNair had had to kill a snake, she used to sit down and cry. Some women did things like that, he knew, not his mother and sisters, but some. He peered around at her again, most uncomfortable. Her sobbing was terrible to see. He felt like a spy. He refrained from going to her, because something warned him that if she had not welcomed him before, she was less likely to do so now, when her face would be distorted with tears. But he remembered that prayer look with hot longing.

He stood hesitating. Presently he looked again. She was just lifting her head to wipe her nose, and she saw him. She gave a little cry and, jumping up, ran into the cabin, and slammed the door behind her. As if he were a robber! Then she came out, even more insultingly, more afraid, and caught up the sleeping baby, and carried her away to safety. She needn't barricade the house against him, need she? Wully thought, angrily. Then he remembered her face in church. He would sit down and wait a while. He would wait till Dod came home, and see what he could learn from the lad. But when he looked again towards the house, there she was, sitting inside the door, and in her hands she had her father's old gun!

How preposterous! How outrageous! If she didn't want him as a lover, she might at least remember he was Wully McLaughlin, a decent, harmless man! Waiting for him with a gun! Could it be that the girl was losing her mind? Her mother had never recovered from that shock of hers. Could Chirstie have been unbalanced by her mother's death! He wouldn't think it! That would be disloyalty. But somebody, his mother, their aunt, somebody ought to go to her by force, and get her away from this lonely place. Who could tell what a girl might do with a gun! One thing he knew, he wasn't going away and leave her there alone, so madly armed, and weeping.

After a while Dod came home, a red-faced, sweating little lad, and sat down contentedly with the soldier in the shade of the barn. He was, of course, barefooted and clothed in jeans, and his fitful haircut did no great honor to Chirstie's skill as a barber. Surely he must know what she was crying about. And he would know that Wully would not be one to make light of her grief.

"What's happened, Dod?" he began at once. "When I came up, Chirstie was sitting on the doorstep crying. What's the matter? Don't you mind her?"

Dod was instantly resentful.

"It's nothing I done." He was decided and scornful. "She won't even let me go swimming a minute. She wants me to stay here all the time. She cries all the time, no matter what I do!"

This was worse than Wully had expected.

"Was she crying before now?" he asked.

"She cries all the time, I tell you." He spoke carelessly. Girls' tears were nothing to him. "She cries when she's eating. She gets up in the morning crying. She's daft!"

"You mustn't say that, Dod!" said Wully sharply. "Can't a girl grieve for her mother without being called daft? That's no way for a man to speak!"

Dod was abashed, but unconvinced.

"She's not grieving for mother," he answered, defending himself. "She's grieving for herself."

This sounded good to Wully. He hoped she was unhappy for the same reason he was.

"How do you know?" he demanded.

"She says so. I says for her not to cry about mother, and she says she wasn't. 'I'm crying for myself,' she says."

Wully had no longer any scruples about finding out everything he could from the boy.

"What's she sitting with that gun in her hands for, Dod? Does she shoot many chickens?"

"Her? She couldn't hit a barn. She's afraid. That's what's the matter with her."

"What's she afraid of?"

"Nothing. What's there to be afraid of here? I don't know what's got into her!"

"Tell me now, Dod!" begged Wully. "My mother would want to know. Does Uncle John see that you have everything you need?"

"That's not it!" exclaimed the boy, proudly. "We have enough. Some of them would come here and stay all the time, but she don't want them. She won't have anybody here. And we're not going to church again." This last he undoubtedly considered a decision worthy of the most tearless girl. Wully, who seized upon trifling straws, saw promise in this. She wasn't going to church again, and she had wanted a good look at him! But what was it—why should she be so silly? Why wouldn't she let him make her happy? She wouldn't need to be afraid if he was with her. He saw that Dod knew not much more than he did about the explanation of his difficulties. But Dod at any time might find something enlightening. Wully coveted his help.

"It really beats all the way you run this farm with your father gone," he affirmed. "When he gets back, I'd like to hire you myself." He saw the boy relishing his praise. "You must treat Chirstie like a man, Dod. You mustn't blame her for crying. It's the way women do, sometimes. You say to her when you go in that my mother is always waiting to do for her. She's the one that can help her. She don't need to cry any more. We can fix things right. You say that to her, Dod, and to-morrow I'll ride over and see what it is. You tell her we'll fix everything for her."

He went away in uncertainty and distress. He ought to tell his mother how things were. The idea of that girl sitting there with a gun, as if she didn't recognize him! Or maybe it would be better to go to his Aunt Libby Keith. She ought to know. He didn't like going to anybody. It was his affair. He couldn't think of insinuating to anyone that the girl was—well, not quite right in her mind. He must be very careful.

And then her face came before him, loving him. After all, it was just his affair and hers. There was some reason why she must wait. But she loved him! His mind dwelt on that, rather than on his inexplicable rejecting. He decided that in the morning he would ride over to the Keiths' and ask in a roundabout way, what the trouble was with Chirstie.

But in the morning he felt so certain that she loved him, in spite of everything, that he announced to his father that he was going over to cut slough grass on his eighty, to use in thatching his new barn, having decided to go to Keiths', less conspicuously, in the evening. This was the first time he had as much as mentioned his own farm all summer. His father was pleased, but his mother protested. Why should he begin such work on the hottest morning of the summer, when he hadn't really been able to help in the haying at all? He might easily be overcome with the heat, in his condition. But Wully, it seemed, was at last feeling as well as he had ever felt. He had been loafing too long. He must begin to get something done on his own place.

So down in his slough he worked away with all his might, and now that his heart was light, and his fever broken, it was no contemptible strength he could exert. About the time he was so hot, so soaked through with sweat that he must sit down for a rest, he saw a horseman coming towards him. And upon that meeting there depended the destiny of generations.

He smiled when he saw who it was. Peter Keith was a cousin of both Chirstie's and his, the only remaining child of their Aunt Libby's and Uncle John Keith's, the smallest adult of Wully's seventy-one cousins, being not more than five feet seven. And he was by far the most worthless of them. Of course Peter would be riding leisurely over after the mail in the middle of the morning, while the haying was to be finished, and the wheat was white and heavy for harvest. His excuse this summer for not working was that he had a disabled foot. He said that he had accidentally discharged his gun into it. Peter Keith was such a man that when he told that story, his hearers' faces grew shrewd and thoughtful, trying to decide whether or not he really was lazy enough to hurt his own foot in order to get out of work. There was no place for laziness in a world where men existed only by toil. It was like chronic cowardice in the face of the enemy. Peter's mother, to be sure, said he wasn't strong. Libby Keith's way of hanging over him, of listening to his rather ordinary cough, her constant babying of him, was what was spoiling Peter, many said. Wully had always been more tolerant of him than some of the cousins were, because he could never imagine a man feigning so shameful a thing as physical weakness. If Peter didn't want to farm, why insist, he argued. If he wanted to go west, to get into something else, let him go. He might be good for something somewhere. But his doting mother would never listen to such hard-heartedness.

The two of them made themselves a shade in the grass, and talked away intimately. Wully was more affable than usual, having resolved upon first sight of Peter to learn something from him. Peter was always full of neighborhood news. Tam McWhee had bought ten acres more of timber, and the Sprouls were beginning to break their further forty, and so on, and so on. Wully was screwing up his courage to introduce the subject that was interesting him, in some casual way. Peter was the last man with whom he cared to discuss Chirstie. But he was exactly the one who might know something valuable. He delayed, the question at the tip of his tongue, till even the lazy Peter thought it was time to be riding on, and rose to go. His foot wasn't really much hurt, but he hadn't renounced his limp. It was then or never with Wully, so he said, trying to appear uninterested:

"I was riding by McNairs' yesterday, and I saw Chirstie sitting there crying. What do you suppose she would be crying about, Peter?"

Peter gave him a sharp look, and grew red in one moment.

"How the devil should I know what girls cry about?" he asked angrily. "It's none of my business! Nor yours, either!"

A cry of frightened anger like that sent an excitement through Wully.

"You know very well what it is!" he cried. "You've got to tell me! It's some of your doings!"

Peter was jumping into his saddle.

"I'll tell you like hell!" he shouted.

"You'll tell me before you go!"

"Let go my bridle! Let go, I tell you! It's none of your business!"

His face told terrible secrets that Wully had never till that moment imagined suspecting. Now he was pulling him down from his horse.

"Let me alone! It's not my fault! Take your hands off me! I never meant to hurt her!" Peter was fighting desperately for his freedom. Wully was trying to control his insane rage.

"Stand still and tell me what it is! I'm not going to hurt you!" he cried scornfully. "What are you afraid of? Don't be a baby!" But his grasp never relaxed. The boy was afraid he would be shaken to death.

"Let me alone! Take your hands off me! Let me go, and I'll tell you! It's none of your business, anyway!" He was free now, and trembling. "I didn't mean to get her into trouble. I wish I'd never seen her! I offered to marry her once—"

He dodged Wully's blinded blow.

"You marry her!" he cried murderously. "You marry her!" The first realization of his meaning had filled Wully with a lust to kill. Peter had sprung away. He gained his horse. Wully ran after him. All the oaths he had ever heard came back to him in his need. He ran furiously after the fleeing seducer. He called after him ragingly.

He threw himself down, too shocked to think plainly. So that was Chirstie's sickening secret! That was why she was afraid of him! That was why she was defending herself with that poor old gun! This was why she had left her uncle's house, and avoided others! Chirstie, betrayed and desolate. Oh, it was well he was trained in killing! He would go after Peter Keith, and make short work of him. He would break every bone in his body. There was no death long enough, large enough, bitter enough, for Peter Keith. Wully lay there weak with rage, crying out curses. Anger, what little he knew of it, had always been to him an exhausting disease. He gave himself up to it.

He was so dazed by this revelation that he never thought how time was passing till he heard the voice of a little brother calling him. It was long after dinner time. Why didn't he come home? His mother was anxious about him. Was he ill? He rose, and stumbled along home.

The sight of that kitchen was a blow to him, so innocent, so habitual it looked, so remote from violence and revenge. The dishes had been gathered from the table. The girls were beginning to wash them. His mother came forward solicitously. What was the matter, she wanted to know. Wully stood blinking. Murder? Had he thought of murder in a place of peace? Instantly he had come far back on that road to his habitual self, when with a shock he came against the criminal fact of Peter. He was ill, he cried. He wanted to rest. He couldn't eat.

He shut the door of his room and sat down bewildered on the edge of his bed. Thoughts of the old security and of the new violence clashed in his mind. His gun stood in the corner. He reached out and took it, and sat fingering it, like a man in a baffling dream.

At length from the kitchen there came a burst of happy laughter. That was his sister laughing. His sister Mary. Laughing. Yes, Mary was laughing, and Chirstie sat there sobbing, sobbing and shaking!

In that unbetrayed kitchen one of the children had said something absurd, that had delighted Mary. He knew that outburst. Mary was a girl safe, and Chirstie was undone. A girl people would scoff at! Not while he was alive! He threw himself down on the bed. He began thinking only of the girl. If he killed that snake, who would Chirstie turn to—who, if she no longer had him? She was alone. Defending herself, fighting for herself. That was what she thought of men! She didn't know any better! He would kill Peter, certainly. But what was to become of her then?

After a while, lying there, he began to see a way out. He saw it dimly at first—it grew persuasive. Peter had been always talking about running away west, had he? Well, he would run away that very night. Either that, or Wully would destroy him. Wully would have that girl, as she was, if he had to fight the whole country for her. His terrible anger still shook him. But there was Chirstie to save, for himself—and for herself. If he killed Peter, what good would that do her? It would make her notorious. The way he saw was better than that. It was an ugly way. But it was safe for her. A situation hideous forced upon them, a thing which had to be faced out, like the war, from which there was no escape but victory. If he got rid of Peter, why should he not have her? Possession of her was worth letting the betrayer go scot free for, wasn't it? She had no one but himself now. And yesterday, in her straits, in her despair, she had turned her face towards him!

By supper time his mind was perfectly clear about the course he would take. He rose, and ate something, excitedly, reassuring his mother that the sun had not prostrated him. He felt all right. He had only to settle with Peter, and then—!

Peter was sitting securely between his father and mother in front of the house when Wully rode up, that evening, and demanded a word with him in private. Peter hesitated. He did not dare to fear his cousin before them. He went cautiously out through the dusk towards him. Daylight was almost gone, but Wully turned his back deliberately towards those who sat casually watching. He didn't want them to see the hate he felt mounting over his face. He didn't want anyone ever to suspect what he was going to do. He spoke to his cousin only a few sentences. Then he turned, and rode swiftly away.

He came to Chirstie's. She was sitting there in the dusk, her head bowed in that despairing way. He gave his horse to Dod with a command, and strode over to where she sat. She needn't try to resist him now. It was useless.

"I know the whole thing!" he whispered. "I've got it all settled." He took her in his arms. She needn't struggle. "It's all right. He'll never frighten you again. You can't get away. I've come for you!"

Dawn found them sitting there together. Indeed, Wully had to urge his horse along to get home in time for breakfast.

The McLaughlins were assembled for their unexciting morning cornmeal, all at the table together, when Wully announced, in a fine loud voice, among them:

"I'm going to be married to-day, mother!"

Her spoon was halfway to her mouth. It was some time before it reached its destination.

"Wully!" she gasped.

"Well, you needn't be so surprised. I am."

"Is it Chirstie?"

Could they ask that!

"I'm that pleased!" she cried. Oh, she wouldn't have liked anything else as well! She looked at him narrowly, with delight. "But you canna just be married to-day, and the harvesting coming on!"

"You bet I can!" replied her American.

Indeed, he never could! Not to Chirstie! They must do something for Jeannie's Chirstie, make her some clothes. Wully scoffed at the idea. She had plenty of clothes, of course. They were going to drive to town and be married, and he would buy her whatever she needed. He refused to listen to them. Chirstie might decide not to have him, if he gave her time.

"Havers!" exclaimed his mother. As if Chirstie didn't know her own mind! That was no way to talk! Isobel couldn't imagine, of course, that Wully had any real reason for such misgivings. Was it likely a girl would not have her Wully! If he would just listen to her a moment, and wait even till the morrow, they would call the friends in and have a wedding worthy of Chirstie's mother. It occurred to him that under the circumstances a plan so respectable might have advantages for Chirstie, if only she would consent. And his father began planning how soon he could spare men and horses to begin hauling lumber for the house.

CHAPTER VI

The McLaughlin house shone ready for the guests the next evening. The light that glimmered out through the dusk came from as many new kerosene lamps as could be borrowed from the neighbors. Inside the house beds had been removed to make room for dancing, though Isobel McLaughlin sighed to remember that there would be at best an indifferent fiddler, not one with a rhythmic dancing soul—like her Allen. Indoors mosquitoes hummed through the light and odor of the lamps, and out of doors they attacked whoever turned away from the series of smudges the boys had built, and were carefully guarding from flame, between the house and the barn. Wagonloads of well-wishers came driving up as it grew dark, and with each arrival the pile of pieced quilts on the chairs in the bedroom grew higher, and the collection of wedding presents in the dooryard grew noisier, and broke loose, and ran, and was pursued with shouts by the assembled half-grown boys. Some guests brought ducks, and some hens with small chickens. Some gave maudlin geese, and some bewildered and protesting young pigs. The Squire gave a heifer calf. The Keiths, poor distracted Aunt Libby and Uncle John Keith, brought two heavy chairs he had made the winter before from walnut.

The bride was not visible. Wully had guarded her carefully, even from a minute alone with his mother, ever since he had arranged her wedding. He told his mother now that Chirstie had consented, she was worried about what her father would say when he heard about it. And because it was so soon after her mother's death. Isobel McLaughlin reassured her. The wedding was the best possible solution of the situation. Let them just leave Chirstie's father to her! She comforted the girl earnestly, being distressed by her face. She hoped in her heart that the marriage would put an end to the girl's newly developed and stubborn depression. She couldn't understand why now that the guests were arriving, the bride should still seem just terrified. No less word described her condition. Isobel McLaughlin could do nothing but leave her with Wully. In his room, where he sat holding her close against him, every time she said, "I can't do this, Wully! I won't!" he kissed her again, powerfully. She must go through with it now, he whispered to her. Even the minister was waiting for them now.

He led her forth, at last, into the parlor. She was wearing the white dress her mother had made for her the summer before, which Mrs. McLaughlin had ironed that day, and freshened with her daughter Mary's cherry-colored ribbons. Wully, harassed by the trivial necessity for respectable garments, was wearing the suit his mother had made for his brother John to wear to college in the fall. It didn't fit Wully altogether, but then, it scarcely fitted John at all. In a space in the midst of their unsuspecting kinsmen they stood, the bride as pale as death, the groom nervously hiding his fear that at the critical minute his bride might altogether reject him.

He kept watching her covertly as the minister tried the patience of man and God by the length of his prayer. He tried to stand near enough her to support her. When the invocations ceased, everyone in the room lifted his head—except the bride. The minister explained interminably the nature of holy matrimony. He exhorted the pair to mutual faithfulness. Wully felt her tremble.

"Will you have this man to be your husband?" he asked at length.

She kept silent. She couldn't raise her head. Wully felt his heart beginning to beat furiously. She was going to refuse him, in spite of all he had done.

There was an awful moment. The room seemed to be hushed and waiting. It was terrible, the length of that moment of silence. At last he spoke forth simply.

"You wouldn't think she would. But she will. Won't you, Chirstie?"

Those standing near heard his words, and as the outraged divine whispered sternly, "Answer!" he bent down and kissed her.

She looked around like one in a nightmare. Her lips moved. The minister accepted the sign. He proceeded with the ceremony. The smile which Wully's words had occasioned spread from those standing nearest even to those who were looking in at the windows—those who pretended to be leaving room for the rest, but were really thinking of their unsuitable bare feet.

The minister had made them man and wife.

The crowd gathered around them. The squire gave Chirstie a resounding smack on her cheek. Girls were pressing around her, the roomful was gathering near her. But she swayed, and fell against her husband, and fainted quite away.

Of course that fainting was altogether the smartest feature of the hurried wedding. Not many hard-working prairie women had bodies which permitted such gentility. It was a distinguished thing to do. The women who saw it forgot for a while to comment on the strange appearance of the bride, which they understood more fully later. At the time it seemed no more than a proper honor to pay Jeannie McNair's memory. When she was herself again, Wully found a place for her out of doors. Planks laid on boxes and chairs made seats for supper out there where the smoke defended them, and since there was no back for her to lean against, she having just fainted and all, it was only proper that Wully's arm do its duty around her. And it was necessary that it give her little strengthening messages, while inside the more zealous young things danced to the fiddle that was not Allen's. Out in the warm starlight and the smoke, the older guests talked to the bride and groom.

Aunt Libby joined them again, when by chance they were for a moment alone.

"Tell me again what it was Peter said, Wully!" she begged.

He felt Chirstie shrinking against him.

"He told me in the morning that he had decided to go this time for sure. I told him he was foolish. And I rode over again to give him some advice in the evening."

Chirstie's hand stirred nervously within his, and he held it more firmly.

"And did he not say where he was going?"

"He only said west."

"That's all he said in his note!" She sighed broken-heartedly. "It's a strange thing he wouldn't heed you, Wully!"

Wully gritted his teeth. "He certainly heeded me that time!" he thought grimly to himself. He had already told his aunt those nicely dovetailing lies half a dozen times, and each time he had felt them crushing his wife. He wished his aunt would go away and leave them in peace. After all, her cursed Peter hadn't got a taste of what he deserved!

Finally the wedding was over. Time, however it drags, must eventually pass. They had driven away together, after he had changed John's good clothes for a fresh hickory shirt and jeans, leaving Dod at the

McLaughlins'. They had had twenty-four hours of the unfathomable luxury of unhindered intimacy. The baby sister was asleep. It was bedtime again.

The new family sat down for prayers. Not that Wully was a man deeply religious. But, as far as he knew, daily family prayers was one of the things a decent man does for his family. They had read that morning, according to custom, the first chapter of Genesis, and that had been most satisfactory, even quite personally interesting now, all about male and female created He them. It had come over Wully with a chuckle that divine commands have seldom been as satisfactory to humans as that first one was. And now, in the evening, he had read the first chapter of the New Testament. He resented that. He wouldn't have read it if he had remembered what was in it. That story of Mary's humiliation might seem ever so slightly to reflect upon his wife. And that right he denied even to the Word of God.

They were sitting together on the doorstep, and his lips were not far from her ear.

"Yon was a strange man, now, Chirstie!" he began.

"What man?"

"That Joseph in Matthew. I fear he hadn't very good sense."

"Why, Wully! And him a man in the Bible!"

"I don't care! He didn't know much! He didn't know enough to take his own lassie till an angel told him! A man like that! He was daft. Or else—"

"I wonder at you, Wully! Or else what?"

"I doubt the lassie wasn't really bonnie. Not like mine!"

A deeper embrace. More kisses.

"Oh, Wully!"

CHAPTER VII

It was growingly inevitable that the news, the determined news, must be broken. Wully, with his whole heart shrinking from the task, made light of it to Chirstie. Wasn't having her better than anything he had ever imagined! He hadn't really known at all at the time how greatly he was enriching himself. If he had been ready then to shoulder whatever blame there might be, he was ready now to do it a dozen times over. He didn't mind in the least telling his parents about it. Accidents of the sort happen among even the most respectable people from time to time. It was in vain that he tried to reassure her. It might be all very well for him to talk so, but when everyone knew about her—Oh, what should she do then! Was it that she doubted him, then? Wasn't he going to be with her? If by chance there should be one neighbor rash enough to see anything not perfect about his marriage, he would tell her for sure there would never be another! It was his mother she thought most about! What would his mother ever do when she heard it? That was nothing! Wully would go and explain it all to her, after his fashion—falsely, his wife insisted on saying wretchedly. His mother would be angry, of course, at first, and give him the scolding of his life. But she'd soon get over it, and come over bringing Chirstie a lot of baby clothes. Chirstie would see if she wouldn't! Why hadn't he explained it to her then, the last time he went over for that purpose, if it was so light a matter? The children happened to be all at home that day because the teacher was ill, and he had got no word alone with her. He didn't add that he had been highly relieved to find them all there. He would go over at once, so that the burden would be off Chirstie's mind.

Having arrived at the scene of his humiliation the next morning, he saw his father coming from the cornfield with his hands and pockets full of chosen ears of seed corn. Wully met him in the path just behind the barn, and they greeted each other without a sign of affection. What did Wully think of these ears? Wully felt them critically, one after another, with his thumb, and found them good. His father started on towards the barn.

"I want to tell you something, father."

He stopped without a word, and stood listening.

"We're going to have a baby."

"'Tis likely."

"I mean—in December."

"December? In December!"

"Yes. That's what I mean."

John McLaughlin's long keen face, which changed expression only under great provocation, now surrendered to surprise. He stood still, looking at his son penetratingly a long time. Wully kicked an imaginary clod back and forth in the path. Presently the father said, with more bitterness than Wully had ever heard in his voice,

"It seems we have brought the old country to the new!"

Wully pondered this unexpected deliverance without looking up.

After a little the older man added, sighing,

"I prayed my sons might be men who could wait."

"A lot he knows about waiting!" thought Wully, half angrily. "Thirteen of us!"

"You tell mother about it, father," he pleaded, knowing his entreaty useless.

"I will not!"

"I wish you would. I can't—very well!"

"You'd best!"

Wully stood watching him tie the yellow ears into clusters on the sheltered side of the barn. He was trying with all his might to gather courage to face his mother. He hadn't felt such a nervous hesitancy since the first time he went into action. He remembered only too well the last time he had really stirred her displeasure. Allen and he had quarreled, and had nursed their anger, in spite of her remonstrances, for two days. He had growled out something to his brother across the supper table, and after that, she had put the little children to bed, and had set her two sons down before the fireplace—it was in the first house they were living then. She had drawn her chair near them, and had proceeded quietly and grimly to flay them with her tongue. She had continued with deliberateness till they were glad to escape half crying to bed. He remembered still how she had begun. It might be natural, she said, for brothers to quarrel. But she believed that it would never again be natural for her sons to quarrel in her presence. And she had been perfectly right about that. What she would say now, upon an occasion like this with her dismaying self-control, he couldn't even imagine. It would be nothing common, he felt sure.

On the bed which she had just finished spreading with a "drunkard's path" quilt, they sat down together in a low room of the second story, where three beds full of boys were accustomed to sleep. She kissed him fondly when he came to her, saying it was a lonely house with him away so much. She wondered why they had not been at church. Was Chirstie not well again?

"I have something to tell you, mother," he stammered.

"I'm listening," she said encouragingly, her eyes studying him tenderly. How beautiful a head he had! How beautiful a man he was!

"We're going to have a baby! In December, mother!"

Over her face there spread swiftly a smile of soft amusement. She had always looked that way when one of her children said something especially innocent and lovable.

"You don't mean December, Wully! Dinna ye ken that? The wee'uns can'na just hurry so!"

He couldn't look at her.

"I know what I mean!" he said, doggedly. "I mean December. I understand." The silence became so ominous that at length he had to steal a look at her. Her incredulous face was flushed red with shame and anger. He rose to defend his love from her.

"You aren't to say a word against her. It wasn't her fault!"

Then the storm broke.

"Do you think I'm likely to say a word against the poor, greetin' bairn!" she cried. "Her sitting there alone among the wolves and snakes, and a son of mine to bring her to shame! I'll never lift my head again!" Her rush of emotion quite choked her.

"My fine, brave soldier of a son!" she burst out, recovering herself. "You did well, now, to choose a lassie alone, with neither father nor mother to defend her from you!"

"Mother!" he cried.

"Jeannie's wee Chirstie!" she went on. "No one else could please you, I suppose! Oh, she did well to die when her son was but a laddie!"

Wretchedly ashamed of his deceit as he was, he was not able to take more of her reproof without trying to defend himself.

"I didn't mean any harm!" he mumbled. "I didn't think." That was what Peter had said.

"And why did you not think!" she demanded, furiously. "Have you no mind of your own! You didn't know what you were doing, I suppose! Oh, that I should have a son who is a fool!"

How terrible mothers are! Fool was a word she hated so greatly that she never allowed her children to pronounce it. It was her ultimate condemnation. He had never heard her use it before. And now she used it for him!

"This is why you have been ailing all summer! You'd reason to be! Did you think you could do evil and prosper?"

He wasn't going to stand any more of that tone. He got up.

"I'll be going," he exclaimed. "There's no place for me here!" No sooner had he used those words than he regretted them. They might seem to appeal to her pity. That was what he had said once when he was a little lad, upon seeing a new baby in her arms, and afterwards, whenever she had shown him a new child, she had reminded him of it gayly.

"Don't go!" she answered, unrelenting. "There is always a place for you, whatever you elect to do. This is a sore stroke, Wully!" Then she added, wearily and passionately,

"When I was a girl, I wanted to be some great person. And when you all were born, I wanted only to have you great men. And when you grew up, I prayed you might be at least honest. And I'm not to have even that, it seems."

He had heard her say that before. He was so sorry for her pain that he hardly knew what to do. If only there had been any other way out! Maybe Chirstie had been right in demanding he tell at least his mother the truth. But he would not! He would share his wife's blame.

"I'm sorry about it, mother," he pleaded. "I'm sick about it. I've done what I could to make it right!"

"To make it right! Do you think you can ever make wrong right! You have spoiled your own marriage. You'll never be happy in it!"

"Don't worry about that!"

"And you the oldest!" she added, suddenly. "I suppose the other six will be doing the same, now!"

"If a brother of mine did a thing like that, I'd kill him!" cried Wully fiercely.

It soothed her to have something not tragic to reprove him for.

"Wully," she said severely, "don't you speak words like them here! 'Tis something you learned in the army! A fine one you'd be to say who should live and who should die! We dinna say the like here!"

"I can't please you any way!" he cried, stung by her upbraidings.

"Strange ways you have of trying!" she retorted. He said nothing. She cried again, presently,

"If only it had been some other girl, Wully! Not Jeannie's!"

What could he answer?

"Mother, you come and see her! She needs someone!"

"Thanks to you! To my son! I won't can speak to her, that shamed I'll be of you!" She thought a bitter moment. "Alex McNair'll be home before December. You'd best come here to me! Wully, if any other mouth in the world had told me this, I wouldn't have believed it! You were always a good boy. Always! Before the war!"

"I've got to go!" he cried in answer. He rushed away, damning Peter Keith into the nethermost hell. The open air was some relief. If only women wouldn't take these things so hard! Well, that was over. The worst part. Any taunt that he might ever have to defend himself from would be easy, after that.

After her unkissed son had gone, Isobel McLaughlin, reeling from the blow he had dealt her, sat with her hands covering her face. Nothing but Wully's own recital could ever have made her believe such a story! It was even thus incredible. If only it had been any other girl but Jeannie's! And her dead! Scarcely dead, either, till her son, betraying years of trust, had shamed her daughter! If Jeannie had been alive, she would have gone to her, in humiliation, though it killed her! Now there was not even that comfort! There was only Chirstie left, and her in such a state! It was not possible to believe her good, beautiful son had done such a base thing! If it had been any boy but Wully! Had he ever given her a moment of anxiety before? Did not the whole clan like him, knowing him for a quiet, honorable, sweet-tempered boy, eminently trustworthy! And now a thing like this to fall upon her! She refused to remember that Allen's irresponsibility, his extravagant pleasure in the society of women, of any size or kind of woman, had made her anxious many an hour. That son, from the time he was twelve, had fairly glowed when there was a woman about to admire him. But Wully had only chuckled over his brother's kaleidoscopic love affairs, things so foreign to his nature. His mother, remembering Allen's escapades, exempted the dead loyally from blame. If Wully had been like that, she might have understood this tale. But he was not like that. He had never been at all like that. It must be the army that had wrought such evil changes in him. That was what had undone her years of teaching. That was what had made all this frontier sacrifice barren. Was it not for the children's sake they had endured this vast wilderness, and endured it in vain if the children were to be of this low and common sort? In their Utopia it was not to have been as it had been in the old country, with each family having a scholar or two in it, and the rest toilers. Here they were all to have been scholars and great men. And now the war had taken away Wully's schooling and Allen's life—and not only Wully's schooling, which was after all, not essential to life, but that ultimate gift, his very sense of being a McLaughlin.

Some Americans might have smiled to know that this immigrant family never for a moment considered Americans in general their equal, or themselves anything common. They were far too British for that. Until lately it had never occurred to them that anyone else might manage some way to be equal to a Scot. Until the war, when some young McLaughlin had shown signs of intolerable depravity, his father had entirely extinguished the last glimmer of it by saying, as he took his pipe out of his economical mouth, "Dinna ye act like a Yankee!" So withering was that reproach that no iniquity ever survived it. Now that that Yankee of the Yankees, Harvey Stowe, had been a very brother to Wully through campaigns and prisons, that denunciation was to be heard no more. But surely, Isobel McLaughlin moaned, her husband and herself had not let the children think that they were anything common. Had she not hated all that democracy that justified meanness of life, and pointed out faithfully to her children its fallacy? She remembered the first time she had taken them all to a Fourth of July celebration in the Yankee settlement, where a barefooted, tobacco-spitting, red-haired orator of the day, after an hour of boastings and of braggings, had shouted out his climax, saying that in this free land we are all kings and queens. "A fine old king, yon!" she had chuckled again and again, explaining his folly to her flock. A man like that had no idea what a king was! He most likely had never even seen a gentleman!

She recalled that Wully, once when he was quite a small boy, had alone and unaided found and identified a gentleman whose team was struggling in a swamp. He was a poor old gentleman, trying manfully to get an orphan grandson to a son's home farther west, and Wully had brought him proudly home, and his mother had "done" for him till he was able to travel on. Having him in the house had been like having a pitiable angel with them. When he was better, they had called all the neighbors in, and the old New Englander had preached them a sermon. He had preached to the children about the Lamb of God, using as his text the lamb tied near the door, and they had never forgotten how gentleness, he said, had made God great. And when he had been starting on, John McLaughlin had taken a bill from his pocket—and bills were things not often seen by the children—and given it to him humbly, for the benefits his presence had bestowed upon the family. Afterwards when his mother had asked Wully how he had known the stranger would be welcome, he had said he knew he was some great man by the way he spoke to his floundering horses. Oh, surely in that wilderness Wully had known the better ways of living. And he had chosen despicable ways! She was only an old, tired, disappointed woman.

If her first-born, that lad Wully, had done a thing like this, what might not the rest of them choose to do! Pride did not let her remember that if the family had been in no generation without a man of more or less eminence, neither had it been without a precedent for Wully's conduct. She was a woman who had sympathy with the mother of Zebedee's sons. If she had been there with Christ, she would have asked unashamed for four places on his right, and for four on his left, the nearest eight seats for her eight sons. What dreams she had dreamed for them! Once she had beheld the President of the United States consulting his cabinet, and behold, her Wully was the President, and Allen the Vice-President, and the Cabinet consisted of her younger lads, even young Hughie sitting there, still only nine, with a freckled little nose, and a wisp of a curling lock straying down from his cowlick towards eyes shining with contemplated mischief. She had felt at the time that such a dream might be somewhat, perhaps, foolish, and profiting by Joseph's distant but well-known experience, she had told it only to her husband. He diagnosed her case in one instant. "You dreamed that wide awake, woman!" She had thought at times that Allen was to be another Burns, a maker of songs for a new country. In her dreams, to be great was to be one of three things, a Burns, a Lincoln, or a Florence Nightingale. And now one dream, her first and longest, was permanently over. Wully was a man now, and a man who brought women to ruin. Sometimes it seemed to her as she lay there moaning that surely the girl must have enticed him into this evil. Then she came swiftly to blaming the whole thing on Alex McNair. If he had come home when he should have, if he had not left the girl unprotected there, this would never have happened. Blaming Alex violated no fond loyalty. In time it came to seem to her that the whole fault was his.

But that afternoon, the small McLaughlins coming home from school found a state of affairs new in their experience. There was absolutely no sign of a baby in the house, and yet their mother was in bed! Once she said when they asked her anxiously, that her head ached. And once she said that her heart was troubling her.

CHAPTER VIII

The autumn seemed to set itself against the house that Wully had determined to have ready for occupancy before winter. Week after week the roads continued so deep in mud that six oxen could not manage to haul a load of lumber the mere twenty-six miles. Chirstie was not as much disappointed by the delay as her husband; she rather liked being hidden away, just then, on the outskirts of the settlement, in her father's lonely cabin. She had seen no one but Wully's mother, and her aunts into whose chagrined ears the humbled Isobel McLaughlin had poured a story as sympathetic as possible, blaming Alex McNair for this fruit of his unfatherly desertion. Mrs. McLaughlin had come at once to see Chirstie after Wully's revelation, apparently utterly pleased over the prospect of a grandchild, never intimating by a syllable that she saw anything deplorable in the unchristian haste of his advent. Her kindness had naturally humbled the girl more than any reproof could have done, and after a long cry the two had been friends, both relieved that estrangement was a thing of the past.

One afternoon late in November Mrs. McLaughlin came as far as Chirstie's with her husband, who was going on to the Keiths' on an errand. It seemed to Chirstie then, and often afterwards, that one who had not seen loving-kindness incarnate in her mother-in-law, had never seen it at all. Her own mother had been a sad, repressed woman, well-loved, indeed, by her children, but as far different as possible from this great, cordial, brimming woman, who seemed so capable of anything that might ever be required of her. One couldn't imagine her hesitating, complaining, broken in spirit.

Chirstie sat beside her sewing, an awe-filled pupil in the things of maternity. It was comforting, when one was feeling daily more wretched, to be assured by the mother of thirteen huskies that a baby is just nothing whatever but a joy, no trouble worth speaking of. Did Chirstie remember that her brother Jimmie had been just Wully's age? Many was the time Jeannie McNair and Isobel McLaughlin had sat together waiting for those two, and sewing, and Jeannie had said so and so, and Isobel had answered thus and thus. Once she had said to Chirstie's grandmother that she wouldn't like to have just a common bairn, and the old woman had replied that there was not the least chance of it, for no woman yet had mothered just a common child. In Scotland, too, when a baby was born, one had to lose the flavor of joy wondering where its food was to come from. But in this land crying aloud to the heavens for inhabitants, there was no anxiety of that sort to dull one's happiness. What had it been to them but an omen of the new home's abundance, that the John McLaughlins had had twins born the year of their arrival, that the Squires had had twins within six months, and that before the year was gone, the Weirs, from the same Ayrshire village, were also blessed in the same way. To be sure, Squire McLaughlin had uttered a word which might not have been taken to signify altogether pure satisfaction with these godsends, the morning after the double increase in his family. He had gone to his barn, and finding that his dearly-bought cow, which was to have furnished him milkers, had given birth to twins, he had sighed a sigh which became a tradition, and murmured, "Bull calves, and lassie wee'uns!" The men had laughed at that, but the women considered it a rather cheap thing of the old wag, even as a joke.

And so they talked on, until the clouds covered the sun again, and they heard the wind rising noisily as they drew near the fire to consider their knitting in the light of it. The elder Mrs. McLaughlin, who was, as usual, doing most of the talking, looked enviously around the kitchen from time to time. She knew she was considered a capable woman. And she had a fine family—yes, certainly, a fine family—in spite of this—affair of Wully's. But she could never keep house as Jeannie did, or even Chirstie. She could, of course, polish her kitchen to some such a degree of luster for special occasions, but to maintain such a brightness was out of the question for her. There had been no white sheets on the wall here for some time now. But each little pane in the window glowed from its daily polishing. The bits of rag carpet seemed always scarcely yet to have lost the marks of their folding, so recently had they been spread down after washing. Even the fireplace was more kept than any other fireplace. The back of it had always just been scraped and scrubbed and whitewashed. Isobel wondered if her son realized the degree of this beautiful neatness.

After a while they heard a wagon drive in, and Mrs. McLaughlin, thinking it was her husband, rose and began leisurely wrapping her knitting. There was no hurry about going. Her man had best come in and warm himself. She stood buttoning her old gray faded coat about her. It had been made, mantle-fashion, in Scotland, before she had grown so large, and she had increased its capacity by the simple device of putting broad black strips of cloth down either side of the front, where it fastened. Afterwards it had needed new sleeves, and hadn't apparently sulked about having new ones of a brownish gray homespun woolen. It had nothing to sulk about, in fact. It was still given plenty of honor as a good serviceable garment. Mistress McLaughlin was wrapping round and round her throat a knitted scarf, pulling it carefully up around her ears, when the door opened....

And in walked—not John McLaughlin, but that tall, gaunt, thin-faced Alex McNair! With those little round, black, piercing eyes shining out from under straight black brows!...

And after him, a woman!

A woman in olive green silk, with black fringe around a puffy overskirt, and such fur and gloves as Isobel McLaughlin had seen only in her travels, and Chirstie never remembered seeing in all her life! The two of them! Coming right into the room!

McNair, seeing Isobel standing there, cried, blinking,

"Weel, weel! You here, Isobel! Weel, weel! This is Barbara, Isobel!"

Chirstie had shrunk in fear and confusion, back into her seat. But the elder woman showed no signs of confusion. She looked the grand wee body over majestically and replied:

"Is't, indeed! I hope she fares better than Jeannie, Alex, dying here alone."

Alex had bent down to kiss his daughter, and seemed to be not so much impressed by this greeting as the little woman was. She continued:

"I have just been sitting a while with my son's wife. You may not remember Chirstie was married, you having so grand a time in Scotland!"

"Warm yourself!" he said to his wife, indicating a chair. "I'll be bringing in the kist." He went out of the door, which had not yet been shut, so suddenly and quickly had it all happened. Mrs. McLaughlin's manner changed at once, and she began helping the amazing stranger out of her wraps. How could those two who watched, so impressed by the richness of them, and so unbetraying of their impressions, how could they have imagined, seeing her, the deceitfulness of those little innocent hesitating airs! The garments were scarcely laid gingerly on the bed until Alex returned, carrying, with Bob McNorkel's help, a great box, which they seemed to plan to leave in the middle of the floor. Chirstie remonstrated and gave them directions. It seemed from Alex's grunting and hard-breathing words as the box was put in the only possible place for it, that he and his bride had ridden out with Bob, who had to be hurrying on. Alex went out of the door with him, and after Alex, Isobel the avenger.

"I'll just have a word with you!" she said to him, stepping inside the barn to be out of the wind. It was a powerful word. Had she not planned it many a night as she lay sleepless thinking of Jeannie and her daughter! "I mind the day you brought Jeannie home a bride," she began. "'Twas no day like this." None of them would ever forget the day she died deserted. Never had Isobel McLaughlin had an occasion worthier of her tongue, and never a stronger motive for making the best of the occasion. McNair was a slow-moving, slow-thinking man, not without tenderness. Isobel's recital of grim detail after grim detail as he stood there amazed, remorseful, humiliated, angry, tired of his journey, and chilled to the bone, overwhelmed him. He could scarcely follow her. It seemed that the whole clan was bitter against him, not only because of his wife's death, but because, some way, his absence had brought disgrace beyond disgrace upon the McLaughlins. He could scarcely understand. Wully and Chirstie had waited and waited for him to come home, and he would not, and fine results these were of his delay! They were married now, but not soon enough.... The girl feared to marry without his permission.... If he had only come when they wrote for him to.... He wasn't to blame the Keiths or any of the neighbors for this. They had done what they could. He was to be very careful what he said to Wully, none too pleased with him, and always hot-headed ... and to Chirstie.... It was all his own fault, he was to remember....

The man was staggered. He liked this news all the less because all the day the little new wife's spirits had been sinking as they traveled over the prairies away from the world. Now to bring her into a disgrace of this sort! He was shivering. He wanted to get in to the fire.

"I have nothing against Wully!" he murmured to the woman who bearded him. "He's a fine man for the lassie!"

Nevertheless, when they were inside again, Isobel watching saw his face darken with anger as he realized Chirstie's condition. She saw too that the girl had seen it, and she determined not to leave the house till Wully would come. She busied herself to make tea for the strange woman, sparing her daughter-in-law with the consideration which so beautiful and so fruitful a woman deserved. She sat herself to make the wee body feel at home. Dod came in from school, and she noticed without relenting the warmth of his father's greeting. Even the little lassie was persuaded to go to his lap. Alex was probably wishing Isobel would go home and leave his family in peace. But she would wait.

McNair was telling something about the passage across when Wully opened the door. He paused a moment, seeing the room full. He looked at them in surprise, and they looked at him with various degrees of admiration. He came from cutting and hauling home wood for the winter and the wind had made his cheeks as red as the fringe of the scarf around his neck, and his eyes as blue as the knit wool of it. In the old coat wrapped about him, he filled the door, a huge young man one would not like for an enemy. His mother had just begun to tell the strange woman that this was her son, when Alex rose and stretched out his hand.

"Come away, man! Come away!" he cried cordially. It was not the kind of meeting Wully had anticipated. But what could he do, with his mother and the women right there, but acknowledge the little woman's salutation, and give his hand to Chirstie's father? And taking his cue from his mother, he smiled so warmly down upon the wee body, that then and there she began liking her stepson-in-law. His mother began at once giving him instructions. He and Chirstie had best begin packing their things. His father would be along any minute now, and they would all go home together. Wully would no longer be needed at McNair's, and with all that work to be done on his own house—

McNair interrupted her decidedly,

"Huts, Isobel! Ye canna take Chirstie away the night!" One would almost think she was the McLaughlins' daughter to hear Isobel! That manipulator of events smothered the retort that came to her, upon this. She simply enlarged innocently upon the inconvenience of Wully's having to ride every day from this place to his own, such a distance. McNair could understand that, but nevertheless they weren't going one step to-night. Wully winked slyly at his wife. He didn't know exactly how his mother had worked it all, but it did him good to hear his father-in-law begging for the privilege of his company for a while— that man he had expected to have such a time with! Isobel yielded gracefully at length. They might stay the night with Alex, but they mustn't stay longer. With her big girls both away at school, she was that lonely for Chirstie!

Then the elder McLaughlin came in and the greetings were all gone over again, with this difference, that John McLaughlin, being less quick at taking hints from his wife than his son had been, showed just enough coldness to McNair to let him see that Isobel's account of the clan's opinion of him was not exaggerated. Naturally after the worthy McLaughlins had departed with so little of the old cordiality, Alex was more eager than ever to placate Wully, who, divining that Chirstie dreaded her father's outburst against her, stood very much upon his dignity, a rather forbidding son-in-law.

When the young two were alone in the kitchen that night, Chirstie said, weary with the day's excitement, and her first taste of shame before strangers;

"Whatever'll she say in the morning, when you're not here, Wully?"

He answered;

"What do you care what she says? Anyway, she don't look like she'd say anything. Just you hold your head high, and she won't dare!"

"It's well enough for you to talk of holding your head high! But how can I?"

"I'll stay about in the morning, and in the afternoon we'll go home. I'll say we must go."

So they planned, little knowing how useless it was to fear the wee body. In the next room, she was saying to her husband;

"Ye never telt me you lived in a sty!"

"Huts, woman! 'Tis no sty!"

"And I thinking you like a laird, with so many fine acres!"

"It's a new country!"

"It's an old sty!" Had she not from the train seen many a little snug place among comforting hills, livable little places! But that had been, to be sure, far from this, in the east. The further west they came, the more they traveled into desolation. Lonely enough places she had seen, but none so unpromising as this sty. Could it be expected that a man with so disconsolate a bride would add to her woe by rehearsing the fresh scandal of the family into which she had come? She remarked at length that it was a terrible thing for a lassie with the baby coming. Why had he not told her of that before? He hadn't remembered to. It was a fine place for bairns. Just let her wait till the spring came. She remarked that it was many months till spring. He snored, more or less successfully.

The next morning the new mother unpacked the great kist to get out the presents she had brought for her stepchildren. She unpacked till the poor room lay heaped high and hidden under richness. Wee Jeannie had a fine doll. Dod had fur-lined mittens. Chirstie had a collar of lace more soft and fine than she had ever seen. And the wee body presented these things with that timid, conciliatory air that made her career later so hard to understand. She apologized for having nothing for the baby. If she had known about that, she would have brought it something good. When was it to be born, she asked, point-blank.

Chirstie, blushing to the unruly little curls about her forehead, said in December. This seemed to relieve her stepmother greatly. By that time, she declared, she could make a fine little dress for it, out of stuff she had in another box. Another box! Were there then other boxes? Of course brides bring dowries to their husbands, the girl remembered with a pang. But she had brought hers only disgrace! But the wee body talked on, in a kindly way. Chirstie watched her making friends with little Jeannie. She liked her, very much. That woman could never be anything but kind to the little sister who was to be left in her charge. Oh, Chirstie could have coveted that woman's love for herself. But, of course, when the truth about herself became known—and when she thought of going to the McLaughlins, to live in that house, full always of children and cousins and visitors, the center, as it were, and rallying place of the neighborhood, her spirits sank lower and lower.

Wully had learned before now to conquer her depression, and he talked the cold hours cunningly away as they rode towards his father's. His reward, that evening, was to see his wife sitting there at the table, long after the meal was over, forgetful of herself, telling his ejaculating mother of the dresses, the capes, the mantles, the ribbons and feathers, reds and browns and greens and blues, puffs and ruffles and tucks, all of these out of one box, and besides the one there were three others left at the station to be brought out, full of—whatever did they suppose? They couldn't imagine! Isobel was trying to fancy how Alex had enticed a woman so obviously rich to the wilderness. She was disappointed in this marriage. She had hoped when Alex married again, he would get a woman who would show him how to treat a wife. But that timid, wee body! Meek like! With faded red hair, and mild light blue eyes! There would be no hope of her ever separating him from the price of a milk-crock! Anyone could see that. The poor wee thing, married to Alex McNair!

CHAPTER IX

Chirstie used to say afterwards, when Wully's younger orphaned brothers and sisters would try to thank her for making her home their own, that she had never spent a happier winter in her life than the one during which she lived with her mother-in-law. That partly explained to them her detestation of all mother-in-law jokes. She would never try to conceal her contempt for any low person—proved low by the very act—who repeated one in her hearing. She had never realized until that winter what a shadow her mother's tragedy had cast over her childhood—until she came to live among the hilarious young McLaughlins. It was as if, set free from the fear and shame of the summer, her life expanded in all directions to make room for the three great loves that came to her—the first and greatest, her redeeming husband, the second, her little son, and the third her mother-in-law, who overcame her by the most insidious kindness, by such a simplicity that the charitableness of her deeds became apparent only upon later reflection. There were even hours when she sang with the children and laughed in such self-forgetfulness that her eyes grew demure and saucy again.

But at other times, if by chance the house was quiet by day, or at night when she was unable to sleep, the shamefulness of her position came back upon her like an attacking pain. The more she grew to appreciate Wully's mother, the more intolerable his deception of her seemed to her. Every time a visitor came into the kitchen, and Isobel McLaughlin stood like a high wall between Chirstie and the possibility of even a slighting insinuation, Chirstie hated more the part Wully had forced upon her. It was the only thing about which she dreamed then of disagreeing with him. She begged him, she entreated him, she really prayed him to let her tell the truth. But he would not. The only way to keep a secret was to tell not even his mother! Some way always he overpowered her with foolish arguments. She wouldn't do just the only one thing he had ever asked her not to, would she? The only one thing that could make him hate her, would be to betray him, now, after it was all over. It wasn't over, not for his mother, she argued. She pointed out that some day it would be all known, some way. It was sin. And were they not to be sure their sin would find them out? How could he grin, and make such an unbelieving face about such a thing! She was helpless before him. He wouldn't even let her talk about telling anyone. Her only comfort was that some time it would all come out. And then he would have to say to his mother that every day she had begged him to tell her the truth! He would have to take all the blame of this unkindness, this cruelty....

It was only a few days before her confinement that one afternoon she sat knitting; in that house of destructive boys not even pregnant hands might lie idle. She had been talking with her mother-in-law about Aunt Libby, whom they were expecting almost any moment. All the neighbors were talking about Libby Keith. She had been away again searching for Peter—in Chicago, this time, on a clue so slender, so foolish, that even the most malicious tongues wagged with a sigh. Her husband, to satisfy her, had gone searching for the son, to Iowa City, and there he had met a man who said that one day in Chicago he had seen a lad in a livery stable, who afterwards he thought might be Peter. He hadn't recognized the boy at the time, only knowing him slightly. And he didn't remember exactly where the stable was. He had been passing an odoriferous door, from which men were pitching out steaming manure.

Thereupon Libby Keith had gone to Chicago. And now she was futilely home again. And she was coming to Isobel McLaughlin to pour out her restlessness. Even winter weather could not keep her at home. She went from house to house seeking reassurance from those who could have none to give. She had had no letter from her boy, and that proved to her that he was lying in some place ill, unable to write. The neighbors scarcely dared suggest to her that Peter might be—well, the least bit careless. Boys were, at times, and thoughtless about writing. But she would never believe that her boy was like that. It was not like him. He would write her, that she knew, if he was able, because he had always been such a good laddie—such an exceeding good laddie that in decency they seemed to have to agree with her. Whoever went to town, went laden with her instructions for inquiry. They must ask everywhere if anyone had heard about a sick laddie trying to get back to his home.

Not a quiet woman, the neighbors reflected. Not one of dignity. One who never would scruple to disturb a world for her son. Some of them recalled Isobel McLaughlin when the news of Wully's death had come to her. They had gone to her carrying their consolation, and she had rejected it with a gesture, going softly about her work with a face that none of them forgot. But Libby Keith took thankfully the crumbs of comfort they saved for her, and begged for more. She humbled herself to ask their incredulous aid. She had no pride left. She had nothing left but her anxiety for her worthless Peter.

She had had three children there in Scotland when her brother John's letters from the new world began stirring her kinsmen. She lay bed-ridden reading them. She had not moved from her bed for two months even when John had taken his departure. Nor would she ever again, the doctors said. She lay there suffering when her second brother, Squire McLaughlin, came to say his last words to her before leaving for America. Then her sisters said farewell to her there, one after another, and her cousins and her friends. And when she would say she would soon be joining them over there, they were kind, and saw no harm in saying that they hoped so. For two years she lay fighting, crying for pain, making her absurd plans. Her neighbors tried to turn her mind away from such wild ideas by ridicule. They hooted at her in disgust. How was she to go to a new place—where there were no houses—nor any doctors—nor any beds! Her brothers wrote her, sternly forbidding her to think of such a thing. But were the children of others to lord it over Utopian acres in a new world, while hers, because she had married somewhat poorly, slaved along in an old one—apprentices of some half-fed mechanic? Her husband resisted with all his might. He was no farmer. He felt no drawings toward pioneer hardships. But his lack of them was in vain. She rose and took him and her three, and journeyed stoutly to her brother's house in Iowa, where she was received with an awe that would have been greater if he could have known she was to die at the fairly mature age of ninety-two.

She had come thus for her children's sake to the new world. Her oldest son, her Davie, a lad well liked by all, was the first of those who fell before the plague of typhoid. That bowed her down. She was nothing but a mother, a woman who nowadays would be called rotten with tenderness. Maternity was her whole life. Then her one daughter married, her Flora, and shortly died in childbirth. These things ought not to be.... Then Peter, who was all she had left to spend her love on, disappeared, leaving in his place a scribbled paper. No wonder, after all, that she sought him through cold cities.

When she came into the McLaughlin kitchen, she bent over and patted Chirstie on the shoulder commiseratingly, sighing a sigh that recalled to the girl all the agony of Flora's death in labor. She was a large woman, heavily built, without grace, and with the long upper lip and heavy face that John McLaughlin and his children had, and keen, deep-set, very dark blue eyes, like theirs. Since that long illness of hers, her heavy cheeks hung pale and flabby.

"So you're back, Libby!" Isobel was constrained to speak to her softly, as one speaks to a mourner. She deserted her spinning wheel, and took her knitting, for a visit.

"I'm back."

"You've no word of him?"

"No word." Each of her answers was accompanied by a sigh most long and deep.

"I suppose you looked everywhere?"

"I went about the whole city asking for him."

"How could you know how to go, Libby?"

"That was no trouble. Men in barns is that kind to a body. I asked them in every one where the next one was, and they told me. Sometimes they drove me in some carriage. And there was the cars. I just said I was looking for my Peter who was sick in some stable. James McWhee went to the police and to the hospitals. There's none better than the McWhees, Isobel. They have a fine painted house with trees about it. They would have me stay longer. James said he would be always looking for him." She gave another great sigh.

"Ah, weel, Libby, some day he'll find him. Some day you'll get word from him, no doubt. It's a fine place, Chicago. The sick'll be well cared for there. It wouldn't be like New Orleans, now. Wully says the lake is just like the ocean. Did you see the lake, Libby?"

"I did'na see the lake. I was aye seeking Peter."

Isobel was determined to have a change of subject.

"They say it beats all the great buildings they have now in Chicago. It'll be changed since we saw it."

"I saw no buildings but the barns. It passes me why they have so many. There was a real old gentleman standing by the door in one, waiting for something done to his carriage. His son went to California in '49, and he still seeks him. He said he would be looking for my Peter. Yon was a fine old man."

Isobel tried to talk about the train, which was nothing common yet. Libby told her in reply what each man and woman in her car had answered when she asked if any had seen her poor sick laddie. Isobel was constrained to tell what one and another of the neighbors hoped about the lost. The Squire had said that he would be coming back in the spring. The boy could never stay in the city when the spring came, he prophesied. Whereupon his mother replied that he wouldn't stay away now if he could by any means get back to his home. And then she wailed, through a moment of silence;

"If I but knew he was dead, Isobel! Not wanting, some place! Not grieving!"

"That's true, Libby. I know that well. I felt that way when I knew Allen was dead. There was—rest, then. No fear, then."

They sat silent. Chirstie bestirred herself guiltily to offer her bit of hope. She felt always in a way responsible for Peter's departure, however much Wully scouted the idea. Wully hadn't told him not to write to his silly mother, had he? Hadn't Peter always been whining about going west? He would have gone, Chirstie or no Chirstie. Wully told her she naturally blamed herself for everything that happened. And she acknowledged that in some moods it did seem to her that she was the cause of most of the pain she saw about her. She began now about the uncertainty of the mails. Didn't her auntie know that Wully never got but a few of the letters that had been sent him during the war? It was Chirstie's opinion that Peter had written home, maybe many times, and the letters had miscarried. Maybe he had written what a good place he had to work, and how much wages he was getting. They considered this probability from all sides.

And Libby's attention was diverted to the girl. Isobel McLaughlin was not one of those, by any means, who saw in Libby's search something half ridiculous. Her boys had been away too many months for that. She had deep sympathy for her, and for that reason Libby came to her more often than to others nearer of kin. But now she did wish Libby would stop asking Chirstie those pointed, foreboding questions about her condition; stop sighing terribly upon each answer. She was making the girl nervous, and in that house there was no place for nervousness. Libby dwelt pathetically upon the details of her daughter's death, upon the symptoms of her abnormal pregnancy. She kept at it, in spite of all Isobel's attempts to divert her until she was about to go. She rose then, and gave a sigh that surpassed all her other sighs, adequate to one oppressed by the whole scheme of life. She said;

"It oughtn't to be. There should be some other way of them being born, without such suffering and pain. With the danger divided between the two. I think—"

But what she thought was too much for Isobel, who had no patience with those who fussed about the natural things of life.

"Havers, Libby!" she exclaimed. "How can you say such things!" And, thinking only of herself and the woman before her, she cried passionately,

"How can you say that it's the bearing of them that hurts! It's the evil they do when they're grown that's the great pain! We want them to be something great, and they won't even be decent! Can you share that with anyone?"

Her words, so poorly aimed, missed their mark, and struck Chirstie. She bowed her head on the back of the chair in front of her. Isobel, returning from seeing Libby away, found her sitting that way, sobbing.

She began comforting her. Chirstie wasn't to listen to what that poor daft body said! Why, Auntie Libby scarcely knew what she was saying. No fear of Chirstie dying. She was doing fine! And well as a woman ever was. But Chirstie couldn't stop crying. She sobbed a long time.

Isobel was putting cobs into the fire when at last Chirstie lifted her red face from her arms, and sat erect, trying to speak.

"I don't care! I might die! I'm going to tell you something!" And she fell to crying again.

Isobel came and stood over her. A fierce hope gleamed uncertainly for a moment in her mind, and went out again.

"What you going to tell me, Chirstie?" she asked kindly.

"If ever you tell I told you, I suppose you'll break up everything between us!" she sobbed. "I don't know what Wully'll do if he finds it out. Maybe he won't have me! Maybe he'll turn me out!"

Her excitement excited Isobel. Chirstie wasn't just hysterical, she saw.

"You needn't fear I'll tell!" she exclaimed loftily. "I don't go about telling secrets!"

"Oh, it would never be the same between us again if he finds out I told you!"

"He'll never find out from me!"

Then Chirstie sat up, sobbing heroically.

"You needn't say Wully's doing evil! He isn't! He couldn't! This isn't any fault of his! It isn't his disgrace!"

"I never supposed it was his fault!" said his mother.

Chirstie never heeded the insinuation.

"I mean—it isn't his! It isn't his baby!"

Years might have been seen falling away from Isobel McLaughlin. She sat down slowly on the chair against which Chirstie was leaning. She could scarcely find her voice.

"Are you telling me it's not Wully's wee'un?" she asked at length.

"It's not Wully's!"

Bewildered she asked;

"Whose is it?"

"I can't tell you that. It's not his."

"And you let us think it was!"

"Oh, mother, I couldn't help it! Oh, I didn't know what to do! And he just did whatever he wanted to. He has everything his own way! He wouldn't let me tell you! Every day I've told him he ought to tell you. But he wouldn't, mother. And if he finds out I have told you, he might even—Oh, I don't know what he'll do!" She sobbed passionately.

Isobel put out her hand and began stroking her hair.

"He'll never find it out from me! Oh, I canna sense it!" she cried. "What ever made him do it?"

"He did it to help me, mother! To help me out! Oh, I wanted him to tell you before we were married. It just seemed as if I couldn't marry him without telling you. But he didn't want anyone to know he wasn't—like me! He says—"

"What does he say, Chirstie?"

"He says he doesn't want anyone to know it isn't his! He doesn't want them to know about—the other one! Mother, I'll make this right some time! You trust me! Some day I'm going to tell how good he is!"

Isobel began kissing her.

"Oh, Chirstie! Oh, you did well to tell me. You needn't fear I'll ever let him know! His own mother! This is the best day of my life, Chirstie!" She rose, and began walking about the house in her excitement, unable to contain her delight. "He never was an ill child, Chirstie! He wanted to help you out, I see. There never was one of the boys as good as Wully, and so gentle-like." She began poking the fire, not realizing what she did. "He'll never know you told me. Don't you cry! I knew he was good. I never believed that story of his! It wasn't like him to do such a thing! It was like him to help you!" She went to the door presently, and called in the children who were playing outside, and when they came in, she took little Sarah passionately up in her arms. "Your mother's young again!" she cried to the surprised child. "Young again!" She gave them both cookies. She comforted Chirstie, stopping in her turns about the room to stroke her hair. She sang snatches of Psalms. "He was never an ill child!" she kept repeating. She began making tea for the girl's refreshment. She looked out of the window. She clasped and unclasped her hands excitedly. She shone.

An hour later John McLaughlin drove into the yard with a load of wood, and Wully was with him. Isobel threw a shawl over her head, and went out through the winter nightfall to meet them.

"Aunt Libby's been here, Wully, talking to Chirstie about Flora till she's having a great cry. You needn't be frightened. She's lying on the bed, but there's nothing wrong with her."

Then, as Wully started hastily for the house, she drew close to her husband. He had begun to unhitch his horses. She said;

"John!"

At the sound of her voice he turned startled towards her. "What ails you?" he had begun to ask, but she was saying;

"Yon's no child of Wully's!"

His hands fell from the horse's side.

"I kent it all the time!" she cried triumphantly.

"No child of Wully's?" he repeated.

"He never done it. I said so all the time! Now she's told me herself!"

He peered at her through the blue half-darkness that rose from the snow.

"Not his! God be thankit! Whosever is it?"

"It's Peter Keith's. Whose would it be, and her in Libby's house half the winter? And Peter running away the very day they were married! Libby's that slack, thinking him such an angel!"

"Did she tell you that?"

"She did not. But I kent it! Did I not say Wully never did so ill a thing?"

"You did not!"

"It was a grand thing for him to do. But I can't think what possessed him ever to take all that blame on us!"

"Can you not?" meditated her husband.

"She says he doesn't want folks to know it isn't his."

"He wouldn't."

"Why wouldn't he, indeed? Would he be wanting to disgrace us all?"

"He wouldn't want folks to know Peter had her. That's but natural."

"It's but natural I shouldn't want folks to think he'd shamed Jeannie's Chirstie."

"So it is," he agreed. "The thing looked well to the Lord, I'm thinking," he added.

"I wish it looked better to the neighbors," she retorted. "This is a strange thing, John." She gave a sore sigh. "Libby grieving herself daft about that gomeril a'ready, so that we won't can say a word to anybody till he's found. Any more sorrow'd kill her. But when he comes back, I'll have her tell the whole thing. She says she's been wanting to clear Wully! She's a good girl, John. But we'll have just to bide our time. I'm glad I've no son like that lad Peter!"

She had had to forget how he had sacrificed her pride for that girl. She had to idealize her son again. She could see that he had done a generous thing. And she would see that the world saw that. She could run to meet Jeannie, now, across the floor of heaven, unashamed. Her husband stood enjoying her face. He said;

"It's early for boasting, woman. You'd best wait twenty years!"

"Little I fear twenty years!" she retorted. A light shone down the path from the house. Wully had opened the door, and shut it, and was coming towards them. She wished she could take him up in her arms and cuddle him against her neck, kissing him as she had done in her youth. She said quietly to him;

"You needn't worry. It's only Auntie Libby that's upset her. There's nothing ails her."

He said anxiously;

"Honestly, mother?"

Wonder welled up within her as she looked at him. There he stood before her, demanding honesty of her, while for months he had been lying great fundamental lies about her very life, which was his honor. "Honestly?" indeed! But there he was before her, beautiful and unrealized, risen to new life in her great expectations for him. She said only;

"Honestly! There's nothing wrong!"

CHAPTER X

Barbara McNair had watched Wully and Chirstie driving away towards Wully's home that afternoon after her arrival at the sty in the slough. It was raining then, and it rained for nearly six weeks. She stood looking after them till they were out of sight. Then she went to the other little window. There she shut her lips tightly—regarded what her eyes discovered, two bony cows, shivering, it seemed to her, in the blown rain, trying to find shelter from the wind by huddling against the haystack that was one side of the barn. The rain was gray and sullen, the prairies sodden and brown; the cows had trampled the ground between the house and the barn into mud, into which they sank knee deep. She stood contemplating. The rain continued blowing about in imprisoning drab veils. Finally she turned away, and sat down weakly. From where she sat, she saw the dripping cows shivering. She sat huddled down. She seemed trying to cuddle up against herself. Her hands, folded in her lap, seemed the only sight not terrifying that her eyes might consider.

Presently the silence of the room was broken with a little sob. She looked up. Chirstie's little sister, standing near the window, was just turning away from it. She had been trying to see something of Chirstie. She felt deserted. Big tears were running slowly down her face. She looked like a neglected, ragged, little heartbroken waif.

Barbara started from her chair. That moment her face showed she had forgotten the surrounding desolations. She ran and gathered the child into her arms. She sat down with her in her lap. The little Jeannie, finding herself caressed, began crying lustily. The new mother kissed her. She caressed her. She soothed her, coaxing her into quietness. She told her little stories. She sang little songs, examining thoughtfully the poor little garments she wore. Dusk came upon them as they sat consoling one another. Barbara demanded help then of the child. Jeannie must show her where all the things were kept which were needed for the supper. They would make some little cakes together. Jeannie grew important and happy.

Dod's eyes fairly bulged with amazement when he saw that supper table. Nothing of the sort had been set before him in that kitchen. His new mother made no apologies. She had been thinking to herself that it had been food of the most primitive sort that had been set before her by Chirstie on the three occasions upon which they had sat down to eat since she had arrived; doubtless Chirstie wasn't feeling very well, and she was at best but a young housekeeper, whose omissions one could easily overlook.

Barbara was pleased with what she had managed to prepare on the strange stove and in the newfangled oven. She saw her husband scowling at the table.

"I dinna like so many cakes!" he remarked severely. One must begin with these women at once, he seemed to be thinking. He had forgotten apparently that his bride came from the very land of cakes, though he wasn't to be allowed to forget it often in the future.

She said apologetically;

"They're not so good, I doubt. I couldn't find any currants in the house. When we get currants you'll like them fine."

"There's too much in them now!" he declared bravely. "We don't have cake every day."

"I do," she said placidly. "I like a wee cake with my tea."

Alex McNair was not entirely a stingy man—not the most stingy man in the neighborhood. He wasn't like Andy McFee, for example, who was so careful of expenditure that when his corn got a little high in the summer he always took off his shirt and hoed the weeds in his skin, to save the wear of the cloth; and who persisted in habits of frugality so that, in his old age, when he rode about in his grandson's Pierce-Arrow, he removed his shoes upon seating himself, to save them from harm, and persisted in this till an able grand-daughter-in-law urged him not to misuse shoe-strings with such extravagance. Nor was he like the elder John McKnight, who when he went to mill always took with him a hen tied in a little basket, to eat the oats that fell from his horse's midday feeding. McNair thought such extremes foolish. He even laughed at McKnight's device. How much easier it was simply to gather the oats up by hand, as he did, dust and all, and to take them home for the hens in his pocket. By this plan the oats were saved, and the hen had a whole day at home to convert useless angleworms into salable eggs. He was not, this proves, an entirely stingy man, yet—the idea of cakes like those for just a common supper! He would have to show that woman his disapproval, his disgust, his sharp pain at such extravagance.

He did his best then, and in the days that followed, to impress her. But she was difficult. She never lifted her voice in perturbation, and she never heeded a word he said. When the howling of the wind woke him up at night, he would hear her sighing, "It's still raining!" When she looked shrinkingly out of the window in the morning, she murmured, "It's still at it!" When he came in for dinner, she would ask, "Does it never stop?" At supper she sighed, like a weary child, "'Tis a fine land, this!"—for all the world as if he was to blame for the weather. She had been housekeeping for him but two days, when he pointed out the woodpile to her. "Bring the wood into the house," she said, as if that was a man's task. "I don't like going out in the rain." "The rain'll not hurt you," he assured her, going about his work. When he came in at noon, the fire was out, the room was cold, and she and the little girl were asleep and comfortable in bed. "I don't like going out in the wet," she repeated simply, as if she had done nothing outrageous in defying him. He had to wait for dinner till the wood was brought in, and dried, and the fire made. The next day she refused, in the same passive, happy way, to bring water from the slough well. She simply remarked she wouldn't think of going so far in the mud, and waited till he brought the water. He never knew that she had hidden enough water for thirsty hours in a jug under the bed, and was prepared to stand a long siege. And then his boots were to be tallowed and dried near the fire. His wife Jeannie had always tallowed his boots. The new wife looked mildly surprised that he should have expected such a duty from her, and left the boots standing, muddy and soaked, just where they were, till he was driven to caring for them himself. And she kept asking him hour by hour, mildly, when he was going to town for her other boxes. She asked him so often, so kindly, that he was forced in despair to attempt the journey through the rain, thinking that maybe if she had something to sew, she would cease making cakes by the hour. And when he started, she gave him a great list of groceries to bring back, and ordered more sugar than his family ate in years. He growled at this—just growled. There had been enough sugar in the house when she came to last till spring. They could not use sugar as if it were water! Why not? she asked, simply. Wasn't he a great lord, with acres? She liked sugar.

He brought back with him only a little sugar, and most of it the coarse brown kind, and a jug of sorghum which was to last till spring. She fell upon her boxes eagerly, and adorned the sty amazingly with rich looking things which never really seemed at home there. She made a new dress for her little stepdaughter at once, and set about making Chirstie's baby a robe. She seemed almost to have resigned herself to the deluge. She spoke with gayety about her ark to the children, and told them to keep their eyes open for the dove. And then, just when she seemed to be getting settled, the winter set in.

Rains she had seen, and could understand, and snows, too, in moderate fashion. But snow like this, continuing; winds like these, whirling darkening wild clouds of whiteness to burst against windows and doors, rocking the little sty as if it were an insecure cradle—winds with horror howling in them, howling all night through the shaken darkness, triumphant, unconquerable winds against which no life could stand—she had never imagined anything like them. She had never before risen in the morning to find doors drifted tight shut, windows banked with white. She had never seen men burrow out of windows to dig open their doors, and tunnel a way to their barns. The well was as distant as if it had been in Patagonia. The newborn calf froze in the barn with its first breath. The men's ears froze, their hands froze, their feet froze. Everything in the house froze solid. The bread had to be thawed out in a steamer over a kettle before they could get a bite to eat in the morning. The milk had to be pounded into little bits and melted. The cold—its intensity, its cruelty, staggered her.

Her work would be done early in the morning, while the men were yet melting snow at the stove to water their beasts—that is, all the work she chose to do. To conquer those long, dark hours she worked away on the baby dress. When it was all finished—alas, too soon for one having endless time to beguile—she looked at it with satisfaction. She had made every stitch of it by hand. It was a yard and a half long, with seven clusters of seven tiny tucks around the skirt, with hand embroidery between some of the rows, and darned net between others. It was ruffled and shirred, and smocked and featherstitched and hemstitched, eyeleted and piped and gathered. And a tiny darned net bonnet, which went with it, was worthy of it. It had taken many weeks to complete it. And always when her eyes were worn by the fine stitching in the flickering candle light, she made cakes, for a change, sparing white sugar with noble economy, using only brown sugar, whatever eggs were unfrozen, fresh butter, and thick cream, and raisins and currants while they lasted.

From the day that Wully took Chirstie home, until the first week of January, Barbara McNair had but one visitor in her prison, and that one was her sister-in-law, Libby Keith. She had to turn to Dod to companionship, which no boy could have grudged to so unfailing a source of cakes as his new mother. His Spartan scorn of the cold brought her, many a time, near to tears. He was anointing his frozen ears one morning, and when she cried out in pity of him, he remarked indifferently that this was nothing. She ought to have seen last year, the time his mother died. With what keen sympathy could she appreciate that story now. She asked without hesitation;

"It was no colder than this, was it?" She couldn't imagine anything worse. Oh, said Dod, they were alone last winter, and his mother and Chirstie had sometimes to help shovel out. But they had had Chirstie's husband, hadn't they, to do that hard work for them? Indeed they hadn't! Dod himself had been the man of the farm. Wully had come but lately. Not lately, surely, she exclaimed. Yes, only in harvest. They had been married right in harvest. He was sure of it. What month would harvest be in this land? she had asked hurriedly. He informed her, and took up his story. He had had to go alone that morning after his mother's death to his uncle's, to get help, and hadn't it taken them three hours to get the sled over the two miles of drifted snow. He told all the tale, even how the little sister was playing alone, and Chirstie had fainted.

All that afternoon there came little words of pity to Barbara McNair as she fondled her little Jeannie; sometimes, when she was making that great, most magnificent cake which appeared unashamed on the supper table, she had to stop and wipe her eyes. Alex McNair had but begun to disapprove of that delicacy when she ordered him so sharply to hold his tongue that he all but obeyed. And after supper, she made him lift down her kists, which because of the narrowness of the sty had to sit one above another in her bedroom. She opened the third one from the top, and took out a dress, wine-colored and soft, and looked at it carefully a long time, examining the seams. Then she sat down, and by candle light began to rip it apart, basque and polonaise and all, to make a dress for the erring Chirstie.

It was the next afternoon that she saw a bobsled drive in. She could see the bundled driver when he was yet some distance from the house, but as he drew near, and stopped, she saw another great beshawled bundle rise from behind the sideboards of the sled. This bundle came at once towards the house, wiped its feet carefully on the doorstep, and, unwrapping layer after layer of covering, revealed itself Isobel McLaughlin. Mrs. McNair could hardly have been more surprised if she had seen an angel descending from heaven. That any woman would be riding around the country in weather like this had not entered her mind. Her concern seemed mildly amusing to her guest, who quickly disclaimed any conduct especially praiseworthy.

It wasn't really cold now, she explained. It was thawing. This was what is called the January thaw. A body can't just stay cooped up in the house all the winter, and besides—and this was the great affair—Mistress McNair would be glad to know that she had a fine strong grandson, born a week ago, the mother doing well! Mrs. McLaughlin had wanted to bring the news herself, she was that pleased! She had stopped, too, at a neighbor's, Maggie Stewart's, who had a baby exactly the same age, a woman whom always before Mrs. McLaughlin had helped through her confinement. She didn't add she had made that visit with the hope of lessening the fierceness of Maggie's slander-loving tongue, though if a good opportunity came she intended explaining to this newcomer the unusual circumstances of the child's birth, which sooner or later she would be sure to hear some way. But no opportunity came. The new Mrs. McNair was so unfeignedly glad to see her, she brought out that wonderful little robe so timidly, that Mrs. McLaughlin had to admire it even more than it deserved. Chirstie hadn't many new things for her baby, because there were so many little things of the young McLaughlins saved for future need. Not that any of them had had so fine a garment as this Mrs. McNair had made. Speed, rather than elaborateness, had always been Mrs. McLaughlin's motto, necessarily. But Chirstie would be that proud of such a little dress! Mrs. McLaughlin could just see her delighted with it. This seemed to comfort Mrs. McNair, who then ventured to show the red dress, all pressed and ready to be put together again, by a method which she hoped would make it large enough for Chirstie—that is, if Chirstie would not be offended by having a made-over dress offered to her. Mrs. McLaughlin again thanked her, and assured her that she need not worry about that. Then Mrs. McNair wondered if Mrs. McLaughlin would take home to the girl her part of her mother's housekeeping things, which the new mother had wrapped and made ready for her. She had divided the few sheets and spoons and cups into two parts, one for each of the sisters—that is, she hoped Mrs. McLaughlin and Chirstie would be satisfied with such a division. Mrs.

McLaughlin, feeling sure that Alex had no knowledge of a plan so bountiful, protested that Chirstie didn't really need the things, that Wully could get her what she needed in the town. But Mrs. McNair wouldn't hear of such a plan for a minute. The lassie must have her share of what had been her mother's. She forebore to mention that she had brought a great deal of household stuff, of a quality much superior to any she found awaiting her. Mrs. McLaughlin, impressed by this spontaneous liberality, began to wonder if, after all, the avenging hand of God might not be seen in this second marriage of Alex McNair.

The hostess was overflowing with questions, the burden of them all being just the one unanswerable one that constantly confronted her—namely, how did civilized persons live through winters of this sort? Why did they endure life in small prisons buried under snow? Had there ever before been a winter equal to this one? And did Mrs. McLaughlin look forward with composure to living through such another one?

Mrs. McLaughlin recalled with amusement and sympathy her own horror of her first winter, enlarging upon her experience. Had not she and her husband and their ten, and the Squire and his ten lived through one winter all together in an unfinished cabin, with a row of beds three deep built right around the walls, and a curtain across the middle of it! Often in those terrible nights she had risen from her bed to go about and feel the legs of her wee sleepers, to be sure they were not all freezing solid. Of course there had not really been as much danger as she imagined, but one of the McKnights had frozen to death that winter, being overtaken on his drunken way homeward by a great storm. That had shocked her until she was really foolish about her children. Her twins had been born that year, too, before the cabin was sealed, and the first snow had drifted in upon the bed where she lay. Fine strong bairns they were, too. The cold didn't really hurt anyone.

Moreover, it drove the fever away, so that they welcomed its coming in the fall, when the whole family would be shaking at one time. Fever wasn't as bad now, either, as it had been at first, though she still fed her family quinine regularly every Saturday during the spring and summer. When the land had all been plowed once or twice, there would be no more of it, 'twas said. And there had been much typhoid at first, before they had realized how much more defilable the new wells were than those in the old places had been. Five of the McLaughlin children had escaped typhoid altogether, which was very lucky indeed, and none of them had died of it, although many of the young ones of the settlement had. These things had all made a good deal of nursing necessary, for thirteen, but undoubtedly the worst days were over. And it was these winters which made the children strong as little lions. Every tree that was planted, moreover, every year's growth of their cherished windbreaks, took away something of the winter's severity. And when spring came, besides, in the glory of that season one forgot the cold, and all one's troubles.

When would spring be coming? asked the longing stranger. Would it be in February, now that January was said to be thawing? No, not February. Nor in March. Sometimes it was a bit springlike by the first of April. But the spring really opened in May. Everyone got out then. Oh, sometimes if the roads were good, the women got out to church in April. Once even there had been a large congregation in March. Mrs. McNair sighed. It was a shame, now, commented her visitor, that she should have had to be alone so much of her first season. If there had been an older daughter, now ... if Chirstie had been at home with her....

Mrs. McNair wondered timidly if Chirstie couldn't come home for a visit, when it got a little less freezing. Mrs. McLaughlin, thinking quickly that Chirstie would surely be happy with this simple gift-giving woman, thought it possible that Wully might bring her over for a few days in March. At least in April.

And when she saw the poor, wee body seize upon this hope of companionship, she felt more sure than ever that Chirstie would enjoy the visit.

If only she would come, that dress should be made for her, Mrs. McNair ventured to promise. And she went on to get more information. What sort of a little house would it be, now, that Wully was building for his wife? What could houses be like in these parts? How many rooms would it have? Isobel explained that there were to be three rooms on the first floor, a parlor, a kitchen and a bedroom, and two bedrooms above. Certainly it would be plastered, all white and clean. Doubtless it would be painted in time, not just at first, of course, but as soon as Wully could manage it. Of course it would have a fence around it, like those Mrs. McNair had seen from the train, and trees, most certainly. They had been planted last fall. Trees were one thing essential on the prairies. Well, likely flowers, too, in time, although women as yet had so much to do that there weren't many flowers about. Mrs. McLaughlin had herself often sighed for a few wee rosebushes. And she had a fine young orchard set out and flourishing. Had not Alex McNair been in these parts as long as the McLaughlins, the new wife asked. And Mrs. McLaughlin, hiding her malice sweetly, didn't doubt but what he would be setting out an orchard soon. "The poor wee body!" she said to herself. "Her wanting flowers, and a man like Alex!"

The pitied one set out such a tea, she sent her guest home with such an abundance of sweeties for her bairns, that Mrs. McLaughlin talked hopefully about her all the way home to her husband. She solemnly affirmed that that new wife would give away Alex McNair's last sock, if she could find anyone to take it; and for her part, she hoped fervently that she could.

That evening as Alex sat smoking his pipe, with his stocking feet well into the oven, his wife asked him artlessly:

"Will Chirstie's man have much, now?"

"What would he have but his land?"

"But he's building a fine house!"

"He would. The McLaughlins were ever spenders and poor. Not that the house would cost much," he added.

"Now what would such a house as his be costing?" It seemed a natural question.

"Four hundred dollars. Or maybe five."

She was surprised, for once, almost excited.

"You could build a castle with your money from Scotland!"

"Likely!" he commented, knocking his pipe's ashes into the stove.

"But a little house like the new one would do me fine!"

"Don't say new house to me, woman!" he roared.

A great deal of good his roaring did him! It was as if she never heard him protesting. "I canna live in a sty," she explained, for the thousandth time, and she said new house to him without ceasing, without haste or rest, by night and by day, apropos of everything he mentioned, till he began to wonder if he were indeed a God-fearing Presbyterian, with such murder in his heart. He couldn't quite beat a woman—a small woman—no matter how utterly she might deserve punishment. He could scarcely do that. But he sometimes wondered if there was any other measure of relief for him. He thought longingly of the silences of Chirstie's mother. He remembered story after story of men who had beat their wives. He experienced a sharp sympathy for them. Doubtless when men do such desperate things, they have adequate reason, he reflected often. He was at his wits' end. He was in despair. That he might have made himself comfortable by granting her request never occurred to him. He was already deliberating upon certain pieces of land he intended buying.

And that woman didn't seem able to believe that he would really buy more land. She simply looked out of the window when he mentioned it, looked out of the window at the winter, and then turned puzzled to look at him, as if trying to fathom why anyone should desire more of such a country.

So February passed, tantalized by new houses, and March got away, maddened by little white fences. Chirstie came over for her visit at home, the first of April, and that first week was frenzied by plans his wife insisted on drawing of her grounds and garden. Alex was no special lover of babies, but he was driven to feigning a prodigious interest in his grandson to escape even temporarily from the meek, eternal din of her ambitions.

Chirstie had come with misgivings, somewhat doubtful of her welcome. But she perceived the first hour in the house that her stepmother was lonely enough to have welcomed the most disgraceful, the most evil of women. She wondered sometimes if she was not dreaming. After all that had passed, how strange it was to be sitting honored in her father's house, coddled, waited on, made much of, by this harmless stranger, who cooked surprising rich things for her delectation, and was making her the most beautiful dress she had ever seen.

She was so happy that she almost regretted that Wully came for her so soon. Mrs. McNair was determined that she must try on the new dress to show it to him. She had forbidden him at first to look in their direction, so he sat with his back to them, holding his little sister-in-law in his lap by the fire. After pinnings and bastings and warnings and ejaculations they had bidden him to turn and look. Chirstie was standing by that window, in the sunshine, where he had first seen her. And now, turning towards her, he gave a little involuntary gasp of delight, more flattering than anything he could have said. He had never seen her before in a soft, rich thing like that. She had worn, of necessity, gray or brown calico garments. And the glowing crimson fabric brought out the whiteness of her neck, the darkness of her hair, the softness of her coloring cheeks, as he cried sincerely;

"Why, Chirstie! You queen! Turn around!"

She turned around for his inspection.

"Goodness!" he exclaimed. "I wouldn't have known you! What'll I do now? I won't can walk beside you in my old rags! I'll have to get some store clothes!"

They laughed for delight.

"What'll I get to match it?" he went on, looking at his mother-in-law. "I ought to have—a purple coat—or something magnifical! Chirstie, do you remember that window! She was standing there the first time I ever saw her!" he explained to Mrs. McNair.

And then at length, in their high, young spirits, they went away, and left her alone there. She was a puzzled woman. A man like that, and a scandal like that! It was incomprehensible. A man building so happily a new house for his wife, with a little fence around it!

That evening Alex McNair gave vent to a great, wicked, blood-curdling oath, most surprising, most improper—all for no reason at all—apropos of nothing. His innocent wife had simply remarked that she couldn't live in a sty.

CHAPTER XI

The infamy of Chirstie's condition, becoming known, had been scarcely less interesting than the scandal of Isobel McLaughlin's attitude toward it. She herself had told her sister and her sisters-in-law what was soon to be expected from the girl, and all her cousins and friends. She had informed them of it casually, without the flutter of an eyelid, as if, to be sure, a little less haste might have been from some points of view desirable, but, after all, Wully's marriage was the one she would have chosen for him if she had had her choice, and the young pair would be happier with a baby. The neighbors had certainly never expected Isobel McLaughlin to "take on" in such a fashion. Some of them had been annoyed at times by her self-reliance, her full trust in her own powers, and were not exactly sorry to hear of this affair which must "set her down a notch." But not a notch down would she go! Her pride, it appeared, was too strong for even this blow. The way she talked about her expectations scandalized the righteous. Maggie Stewart said one would have supposed Wully had waited ten years for that baby.

It had been bad enough in the beginning, but after the child was born it grew out of all bounds. Her husband's younger sister, Janet, a woman still of childbearing age, came to remonstrate with her. For the sake of the other young people in the community, to say nothing of her own family of half-grown boys and girls, she really ought to moderate her raptures somewhat. She was just encouraging them in wrongdoing! But Isobel replied simply that since she had always had to be painfully modest in praising her own children, she was going to say exactly what she thought about this grandchild. She philosophized shamelessly about the privileges of grandmothers. And, after all, if she was his own grandmother who was saying it, Janet would have to acknowledge that the baby was an unusually fine child.

Janet did have to grant that. She was the first one, too, to notice the remarkable resemblance the child bore to his father. Isobel was grateful to her for that hint, and after that day no visitor departed without agreeing that wee Johnnie was a living picture of great Wully. Isobel would recall her son's infant features. Wully's nose had been just like that. And his eyes. She minded it well, now. This child brought it all back to her. She had occasion to repeat these reminiscences, for baby-judging, giving a decision about his family traits, was nothing less than a ritual among these Scots. A woman could hardly acquit herself with distinction in it with less than six or eight of her own. And men, even fathers of thirteen, knowing how far short of the occasion they would come, generally avoided it as best they might.

Squire McLaughlin, of course, was just brazen enough to enjoy such a ceremony. He may have had some secret sympathy for Wully's predicament, for he came over to inspect the child only a few days after it was born. The Squire was the playboy of the community. None of them ever took him seriously, and none failed to welcome him heartily in for a "crack." It appears that even his absurd pretensions endeared him to his friends. He fancied himself a great lord, before an acre of his "estate" was subdued, and sang a silly song about gravel walks and peacocks. He never hauled a load of gravel to fill the mudhole before his cabin door. But he did the easier thing. He managed to have some gullible soul send him a pair of peacocks. They died promptly upon arrival. He said, laughing with the neighbors at himself, that it was the shock of seeing their laird barefooted that killed them. He was a farmer who rode forth to preside at theorizing agricultural meetings, while the forests of weeds on his land grew unchecked up to the heavens. (Even two years ago, the wild sunflowers near a culvert on that farm reached the telephone wires.) He was later on one of the first men west of the Mississippi to have pure-bred bulls, and east or west, no man confused pedigrees more convivially. From the first he considered it his duty to see that no Scottish folly was forgotten in the new world, or even hogmanay allowed to pass unobserved. He was the man who all but popularized curling in the west. Three times he had been left an undaunted widower with a family of small, half-clothed children, his esteemed heirs and heiresses of only his gay fancies. Just now he was looking for a fourth helper to relieve him of the responsibilities of his family, and such a man he was that, in spite of his follies, all wished him success in the venture. He consulted Isobel about various possibilities and she gave him her opinion, with the frank statement that she pitied any woman who married him. However, he still liked her. He had always liked her since that time in Ayrshire, soon after she had married his older brother, when she had saved him from a long and well-earned term in prison for poaching. His successful pursuers were almost upon him when they turned suddenly in the wrong direction, from which they had just heard firing. She had seen his plight, and fired cunningly into the air, and when the men had rushed into her cottage they found only a young woman demurely sewing on baby clothes. Now since, of course, it was impossible to poach in a land where not even God preserved game, he was a reformed man, and an eminent huntsman. But sometimes he still said jovially that he might as well have gone to prison as to have to listen to all she said to him on that occasion. Even yet he was not averse to giving her occasions of finding fault with him.

So when she lifted the baby up for his inspection, he rose, and squinted down thoughtfully upon the little bundle. He turned his head appraisingly from one side to the other. Then, knowing very well what she thought, he said recklessly;

"He's a perfect little McNair, Isobel. He's like Alex. That nose of his—"

She enlightened him stoutly. He persisted in his error, and only asked:

"What's he called?"

Now what to name the child was a question not altogether easy for Wully, who had been standing near his mother, looking with proper paternal pride upon the child. Each McLaughlin named his first-born son, not boastingly, for himself, but gratefully, for his father; so that Johns and Williams came alternately down through the generations. That was the rub. Perhaps John McLaughlin might not relish having this irregular child bear his name. So Wully was too proud to seem to desire it.

"He's such a husky little fighter for what he wants, we thought we'd call him Grant. There's no better name than that, is there?"

His father was sitting by the stove, smoking, seeming as usual absorbed in a dream and only half-conscious of what was going on about him. At this he took his pipe from his mouth and said, without a sign of emotion;

"I wonder at you, Wully. The laddie's name is John."

Wully was greatly relieved.

"Oh, well," he said lightly. "Maybe that would be better. There won't be more than fourteen or fifteen John McLaughlins about in twenty years. Grant'll keep. We'll save it for the next one."

Wully had rejoiced beyond measure at the child's birth, not for the reason some supposed, but solely because Chirstie was safely through her ordeal. So gay he had become, so light-hearted, after that burden of anxiety for her had been taken from him, that he seemed quite like a rejoicing young father. It had been terrible for him to see her time unescapably approaching. Those days seemed to him now like a nightmare. He had planned what he would say to his wife when he adopted her baby for his own. He would go blithely in, and cry to her gayly, "Where's my son, Chirstie?" And the child would be his. He had planned that. But it had been different. That one irrepressible moan he had heard from her before his mother had sent him for the doctor had driven him through the night cursing. Cursing that man, whose very name he hated to recall, cursing any man who lightly forced such hours upon any woman— to say nothing of a dear woman like Chirstie. He wanted to kill such men, to pound them to bits. And yet, lightly or not lightly, what would his love of her bring her to, eventually, if not to such hours as these! It was a hellish night. Afterwards he had gone in to see her, not blithely, but otherwise. He had found her lying there, hollow-eyed, exhausted, all her strength taken from her, and her roundness, leaving her reduced, it seemed, to her essential womanhood. And then suddenly he had not been able to see her for the tears that burned his eyes. He had knelt down beside her, to put his face near hers, so unseeing that she had cried sharply, "Don't! Be careful!" He had hurt her! But her hand was seeking for his. When she had shown him the child—well he remembered that she had never asked him for pity for herself. But now her eyes were praying, "My baby! Love my baby, Wully!" With her lying there, even her familiar hands looking frail, her hair lying wearily against her pillow, if she had asked him to love a puppy, would he not have bent down to kiss it! Later he had marveled to see her with the child. A farmer, a man judging his very female animals by the sureness of their instincts for their young, he wouldn't have wanted a wife not greatly maternal, he told himself. It came to be soon that in loving the child he was playing no rôle; he liked all his wife's adornments.

So the terrible days passed away. His wife became altogether his. And wee Johnnie slept and thrived, his tiny hands doubled against his little red face, in the cradle that had served the five younger McLaughlins. When he opened his bonnie blue eyes, he saw only adoration bending over him. He felt only delighted and reverent hands lifting him. His grandmother, who "just couldn't abide a house without a baby in it," would sometimes allow one of her children, sitting carefully in just a certain chair, to hold him a little while as a mark of her favor. If Johnnie was a shame to the household, he was certainly an entertaining and a well-fed shame; if he was a disgrace, he was surely an amusing and a hungry one.

It was wonderful how completely Chirstie was sheltered from reproach. Though her humiliation was gossiped about by the hour, after all, the gossipers had to remember her mother, and, sighing, grant the daughter some little toleration. And then, however proud that Isobel McLaughlin might be, there was hardly a family in the community which had not, upon arriving from the old country, made "Uncle John

McLaughlin's" their convenient home till another could be built. Moreover, Wully had always been particularly indulgent to those who were his aunts and uncles. Greatest of all, he was a soldier. Not so far down the creek, a Quaker soldier had come home from war without a leg, and his congregation had said if only he would say, even privately, that he was sorry he had fought, he would again be received into their communion. But he refused to say he was sorry. And they refused to take him again to their approval. That didn't seem to trouble the soldier very much. But it had troubled the Scotch, where he had come to work, extremely. They loved to belittle the Quakers for what they considered a meanness to a man who had fought. So it behooved them to treat their own veterans with more consideration. On the whole, there might have been much more gloating than there was. There might have been battles. Great, quiet, simple men like Wully, however, people seem instinctively to avoid exciting to fury.

So Chirstie had scarcely had occasion to feel the awkwardness of her position till the afternoon early in April when her stepmother came over with the finished dress to try on her. Chirstie had donned the beautiful, rich, wine-colored thing, to be sure it hung right, and set right, and standing forth so that Isobel McLaughlin might view the effect, she turned round and round while Barbara McNair smoothed out even imaginary wrinkles. It was pronounced perfect. Mrs. McNair admired it as if it were not her skill but the girl's beauty that made the gown remarkable. Then, beaming, as much as her little pale weak face could beam, she unwrapped a hat—a hat all wine-colored and black, and set it jauntily on Chirstie's head, so that the long feather swept down over the brown coil of hair low on her neck. Chirstie was radiant. She had never seen so lovely a hat in her life, she said. And she stood looking at herself in the little glass, in surprise, a very happy surprise, to see how she looked in such soft, rich things. Then, with a command, Barbara McNair took all the joy out of her face.

She simply demanded that Chirstie wear that conspicuously beautiful outfit the second Sabbath to come, when the winter's crop of babies was to be formally dedicated to the Lord. Chirstie went suddenly crimson, standing there, blankly, fingering the feather on her neck.

Mrs. McNair insisted on an answer.

"Oh!" cried Chirstie meekly, her eyes appealing to her mother-in-law. "Our baby—" she began to say it wasn't to be baptized, but she had to turn away. She started for her room, to take the dress off.

The girl was so sensitive, Isobel started to say—But Barbara called after her to come back, breaking forth into the broadest Glasgow accent. They weren't to suppose she didn't understand! She had known it all the time. That innocent laddie had told her, unconsciously. (More innocent then than now, she might have added, if she had known.) And she thought, indeed, that Chirstie had great reason for shame, and not of her bonnie wee Johnnie, either, but of her own heathen ingratitude. Chirstie lifted her face upon hearing that, from the towel upon which she was wiping it, and Mrs. McNair demanded that moment if she expected the Lord to sit studying the almanac all the year for her convenience. She was sure that if she had been in Chirstie's place, and the Lord had given her a son, she wouldn't have gone sulking, no matter what the month might have been. Was it not better to have one any time than none at all? she demanded, with such a passion of regret for her own childlessness that Chirstie was left speechless. She had never imagined anyone speaking in such a strain. She looked at her mother-in-law, who seemed mildly amused. The idea that she had been deriding the Lord's chronological calculations was in itself sobering to one of so tender a conscience. The giver of all her good clothes went scolding away at her, till she promised at least to wear the new things the week after the baptisms.

Chirstie kept thinking of the scolding as she drove in the wagon of that harassed man, Alex McNair, with her stepmother and her mother-in-law, to see the new house that was getting about ready for her occupancy. Wully had to lay a plank for a walk hurriedly from the wagon to the house, for the new Mrs. McNair still wore such boots that one step in the thawing black mire would have ruined them. It was always that way. That little insignificant-looking person refused to adjust herself to the new country. She just sat tight, and let the great significant country adjust itself to her as best it might. The house towards which she neatly walked was not perhaps, to disinterested eyes, a very inviting place. But to Wully and Chirstie it was their very palace of love. It stood a story and a half high on a slight rise of ground, a decent way back from the path that has since become one of the nation's highways, built of shining new lumber, the tall grass around it trampled into the black ground littered with bits of boards and yellow curling shavings. From the front door, just hung that day, the women looked down over fifteen miles of prairie, an occasional plowed square humanizing the distances, which sloped with so gentle an incline that one standing on any one of the acres could scarcely have told it was not level. From the windows of the parlor the women saw the plot that Wully's father had insisted on breaking the year before, along one side of which the maple seeds he had planted were presently to appear as slight as spears of sprouting grass. From the kitchen window they saw a row of elms as thick as broomsticks, which Wully had brought the fall before from the creek. In a long furrow there, the walnut trees that were to make gunstalks for the World War were still waiting in their shells for a warmer sun to bring them forth, and to the north the trench was ready for the red and white pines that are nowadays a pride to the family. Chirstie pointed to the piece of ground that was to be fenced for a garden. Whereupon Mrs. McNair asked anxiously if the fence was to be painted white.

Wully heard his father-in-law move impatiently behind him, and, though he hadn't before thought of such a thing, he answered that it would be painted white as soon as he had the money for the paint. The stepmother-in-law sighed with relief, and began inspecting the kitchen closet. Wully pointed out with malicious glee the finish of the cupboards, making light of the expense and difficulty of building, while his father-in-law poked about glooming, refusing to admire the conveniences which the little woman coveted with so gentle a simplicity. He still had a grudge against that man, and aired it whenever he could without Chirstie seeing him. He knew McNair disapproved of the size of the windows. But what business of that man's was it what his windows cost?

The Sabbath of the Communion Wully unabashed, and shame-filled Chirstie wearing the appealing old coat of her mother, and the bedecked wee Johnnie went to church for the first time since the baby's birth. But let no one suppose that they attracted much attention. What chance for consideration could even the most unholy child have had that morning, sitting in front of the Glasgow fashions in the person, or on the person, of his stepgrandmother? Wasn't she wearing a most stunning little hat with a dark green feather curling down over a chignon of red hair, sitting there in the pew just behind Mrs. McLaughlin, who wore with grace and satisfaction the bonnet a lamenting friend in Ayrshire had made for her in fifty-four, and just in front of Mrs. Whannel, whose headpiece was conceived in the spring of fifty-eight, and across from Mrs. McTaggert, who had bought somewhat more expensively than was necessary in sixty-one, but who, considering the well-preserved condition of her purchase, had really nothing to regret. One skilled in millinery might have reckoned from the mother's bonnets more or less accurately, the year of each family's immigration, although the array of such young girls as were not away at school would have slightly vitiated his calculations. And now, this Sabbath morning, there sits down in this world, so remote from others, a Metternich jacket, a cape-like affair trimmed with fur, and a skirt spreading gracefully, but without hoops, a floating veil, and gloves embroidered in faint gray! If wee Johnnie had been baseborn twins, he could never have attracted more than a stray thought to himselves on that occasion.

CHAPTER XII

Soon after the garments of Barbara McNair dawned upon the congregation, her husband bought three hundred acres of land at three dollars an acre. There are those who say a man owning eight hundred and forty acres of land should be happy. Alex McNair was not. There was in his flesh one great thorn— that Glasgow wife.

She had lived through the autumn and the terrible winter, waiting for spring. And now that spring was here, what was it? Only an oozy wet waste, with patches of green in the lower places, and winds shrieking always across flat desolations. Near the sty, a sagging haystack of a barn, and a couple of bony cows trampling dead grasses deeper into the mire of the dooryard. If only there had been even a little white house, and a fence, and a few flowers sending up their endearing shoots! But this! And her from Glasgow!

Words failed her.

Had she not set forth day by day and hour by hour conscientiously, the necessity of a new house? Yet in the face of her demands, her man had gone to town to buy more wilderness. If she had known that spring that Dod was to sell part of that land for six hundred dollars an acre, her contempt for her husband's folly would scarcely have been less hot. There he was, driving into the yard now! She went to the door and greeted him.

"You didn't buy it?" she asked.

"Did I not say I would buy it?" he answered doggedly.

Not a change of expression passed over her face. She stood watching him unhitch his team. She had never before been so much interested in that process, having always avoided the barn.

The next day, when he was in the field, and Dod was hitching up, she went out and watched him. Would he show her how he did that? she asked. She thought she ought to know, she said. Which were the gentlest horses? And which harness did they take? She learned where it all hung in the barn. Dod liked teaching an old person. It wasn't any trick to hitch a horse to the wagon, he said. You put this under the belly, so. And the lines through here, taking them from here, thus. She practiced. She grew proficient. She waited.

One day in early May her husband rode away horseback to the Keiths', to pay back one of the many days of labor he owed that family. He left home at daylight, and Dod went to school. Then Barbara began.

When McNair came home that evening, Dod asked, lonesomely,

"Where's mother?"

"Is she not here?"

"She is not."

"She'll be gone to Chirstie's. Or McCreaths'. Who came for her?"

"She took the team and went herself."

"You're daft! Her take a team!"

But the team was gone. The barn was as empty as the house. Dod made a fire in the fireplace, and put the kettle on. Then the father made a discovery that the son had made some time ago. The cupboard was bare. Not a bite in it. Not a crumb of cake.

McNair didn't like that. She might have told them where she was going. She ought to have come back in time to have the supper ready. He hated a cold house. He went to his tobacco box. At least that was always ready for a hungry man. He opened it, and found a strange white paper in it. A note from his wife. A fine note! "I can't live in a sty," it said. "I have gone back to Scotland. Jeannie is with Chirstie. Barbara Ferguson."

Back to Scotland!

A woman alone!

Starting away with his team! She was daft! He rushed into the bedroom, as soon as he began to realize her meaning. Were her hat and cloak there? They were not! What was this? The kists not one on top of the other, as usual! Spreading all over the room! And empty! Nothing left in them! He rushed to the kitchen. The kist that set there was empty, too, more empty if possible than the others! He sat down.

He was outraged. He was speechless. That woman hadn't been able to lift those boxes alone into the wagon, so she had taken all their contents and left them. Such cunning! Such deceit! And had he not paid all her passage from Scotland! She had left him! Left him, Alex McNair! Without saying a word! Her so quiet, and all! The whole clan would know all about it! They would all have seen her passing! A woman alone! Had anyone ever before heard of such a thing? Certainly not in those parts! Everybody wondering where his wife was off to! Oh, Jeannie would never have played him so base a trick!

Dod came into the room. McNair stuffed the note hastily into the box.

"Your mother has gone to town," he murmured, meekly.

Dod heard that with surprise. Presently he volunteered that he saw now why she had wanted to learn how to hitch up the horses. Had she indeed learned all that from him? his father gasped. Oh, the depth of deceit in her! And he had paid her way from Glasgow! Dod made disconsolate cornmeal for their supper, forgetting to put salt in it. To think of that woman ridding the cupboard of its last crumb! McNair went to the barn and pretended to work, after the meal, being too excited to sit still. Back to Scotland! Had ever anyone heard the like! Everyone would be laughing at him. A rich wife, indeed! Oh, he understood now why the canny widowers of Scotland had meekly let him take this jewel of a woman away to America. They must have known her!

There was but one thing to be done. He would rise early, long before dawn, and pursue her, getting out of the neighborhood before anyone would be awake to see him pass. Her with his good horses in the town, not knowing enough, maybe, to give them a drink at the end of the journey! If she ever imagined he would give her a cent to get back with, how greatly mistaken she was. He would surely show her who was master here.

He found her the next afternoon, in the hall of one of those long, shanty-like hotels which comprised the town, found her in the very act of making a bargain with a man to make her new boxes to take the place of those she had so extravagantly abandoned. They faced each other in her room, he, tall, gaunt, black-eyed, ragged, she, small, dainty, red-haired, bedecked. Her placidness, as usual, disarmed him. He began;

"You can't go back to Scotland! Are you daft?"

"I canna' live in a sty."

They were off, then. He urged decency, morality, economy, honesty, pride, race, the waning reputation of Glasgow. After each argument she simply said, like one born foolish;

"I canna' live in a sty."

It was a deadlock, till he demanded angrily where she expected to get money for the journey. At her answer he surrendered. It fairly took the life out of him. She certainly had not expected to get it from him, thank you! She knew him too well. She had money enough with her to take her comfortably to her home in Glasgow. Did he suppose that she was one to come to the wilds without knowing how she might get back? She had kept it all—all that gold, mind you!—in the lining of her muff.

That woman had come thinking she might not stay! He, Alex McNair, had been, as it were, married on probation. And him a Presbyterian!

He asked hopelessly what kind of a house she wanted.

She replied promptly that she wanted three good big rooms downstairs, and two upstairs, a wee porch, all painted white, except the green shutters, with closets and windows like Chirstie's and besides a wee white house for the fowls. All this was to be bought to-day, at once.

The Lord preserve us! Why, there wasn't a painted fowl house in the state!

The train left for Glasgow at seven the night.

He couldn't buy all that in a day, could he? He had no money!

He could sell the last great plot he had bought.

Was she daft? Did she suppose he could sell it in a day?

Why could he not sell it in one day? Hadn't he bought it in one? She would call to the man to bring in those boxes.

He would buy the lumber as soon as he got around to it. Couldn't she trust him to do it?

He hadn't told her in the first place that he lived in a sty, had he? She felt the inside of her muff carefully.

The next day in the dusk they drove into Wully's together, having a wagon whose strange shape would have excited the curiosity of the most philosophical, with that same long, uneven thing all covered with blankets and tucked in, such a load as no man ever hauled, and plainly the same thing that she had taken with her the day before. McNair was apparently in a bad humor. How could the two who came out to welcome them in, know that the nearer he had got to his home, the more he dreaded the explanation he would have to give of his wife's desertion. But he had not yet learned all the depth of that lintie! Was she embarrassed? Not she! She began immediately telling the news, in that hesitating, ingratiating way of hers. They were to have a new house! The lumber was to be hauled at once. She was that glad she hadn't been able to wait for Alex, but had gone in ahead, to see about it. It was all settled. Just about like Wully's, it was to be. But a little larger. With a white fence. And a wee white fowl house. They had bought even the paint. And, having had some time on her hands, she had found this wee pair of shoes for the baby. No, they couldn't come in. Let Wully just hold wee Johnnie up till she would see if they were the right size. Out of that confounded muff came the shoes. They fitted. Well, the McNairs would just take their wee Jeannie and be going on. She had so wanted them to hear her good news. She hoped Jeannie hadn't troubled Chirstie much. And wasn't Johnnie just growing bonnier day by day!

What could a man do in the face of that? Where in the name of the shorter catechism had the woman got those shoes, and when—after all the money she had wasted that day on houses? McNair simply gave up. Like the Queen of Sheba before Solomon, he had no spirit left in him. But he had acquired an uncomfortable amount of fear of women.

Chirstie and Wully took it for granted that the rich wife had paid for the house, until the next Sabbath. Therefore, when Wully heard as he came out of church that his revered father-in-law had sold part of his newly bought land to Geordie Sproul, in a panic so to speak, in a hurry, without much bargaining, to get the required funds for the lumber, he grinned to himself, and waited to hear his mother's comment on the tale. He took his family as usual home to his mother's, after the service, and when dinner was over, he had a chance to speak with her alone. She heard his pleasant suspicions. Doubtless the new wife had made him sell that land. And she chuckled with deep, deep mirth.

"Yon's a fine woman, Wully!" she exclaimed, relishing her thoughts. "She's a grand wee captain!" She heaved sighs of contentment from time to time all the afternoon, whose import was not lost on her son. Surely, late as it was, Jeannie was being avenged.

Quite unconscious of the envious comment and the snickers of admiration which her house was causing among her neighbors, Barbara McNair went again with her husband to town, a month later, after the bluebells had faded in the creek woods, just when the wild roses were beginning to bloom, when the prairie was blue with spider lilies. She rode along arrayed like the lilies—not to say like the twenty-eight colors of wild phlox which a Dartsmouth botanist records he found there that year. When at length she came within sight of the town which stirred Isobel McLaughlin so greatly to speculation, she speculated upon it not at all. There was nothing significant to her in a town of eleven real estate offices and nineteen hotels, wherein every other inhabitant was a land speculator. She left the main street without paying it the compliment of a thought, and turned toward the first street of dwellings, a muddy lane not worthy to be called a street. The further down it she went, the more homesick she grew, so bare and naked it was, shack after shack uncared-for—wherever she turned, no gardens, no flowers, no trees, even in the year's height of leaf and blossom. On she went, down one path after another. Then, away at the end of one—Oh, there she found a little, unpainted vine-covered shanty, with color, with fragrance, iris blooming, borders of clove pinks, pansies, a yellow rosebush, a red one, grapevines in blossom, a honeysuckle, budding peonies!

It came over her with such delight that it never occurred to her to hesitate. She pushed open the gate, and followed the path of clove pinks around the house. There in the shade a woman was bending over her washtub, a large, fat uncorseted woman, who raised a red face from her steaming work.

Barbara said to her positively and politely, moved to her broadest accent,

"I have come to see your flowers!"

The woman wiped her well-soaked hands on a limp apron, and replied in perfect Pennsylvania Dutch;

"I don't understand you." But she smiled a smile of extraordinary width.

They faced each other, Scotland and Germany, curiously for one moment. Then Barbara pointed dramatically at the pansies. There was that look on her face that was understood by frontiers-women of many tongues. The German began babbling sympathetically about her display, pointing out one beauty after another, breaking off little sprays to hold near her visitor's longing nose. So much there was that Barbara wanted to ask, and her hostess wanted to explain, and they understood each other after so many repetitions and efforts! Barbara examined each plant, and felt the soil it grew in. She bowed her face down to them again and again, hungrily. Not one did she omit to sigh over enviously. Presently the German led her into the shanty, and set before her in a red-carpeted, closely-guarded parlor, coffee and coffee-cake, which Barbara esteemed but lightly, surprised out of politeness by the fact that on the kitchen table a pair of pigeons sat cooing. Then, the refreshments being finished, the woman took her by the hand, and led her out of the house, down a barren street, just as she was, in her wet dress, unhatted, red-faced. Barbara surmised she was being taken to a place where plants were sold.

They came to a large square house, built on a high foundation, in a yard planted with trees which were not just small sticks, approached by a walk which had wide blossoming borders which Barbara would fain have examined. But her guide waddled up determinedly and knocked on the door. A lady opened it, a lady perhaps fifty, whose gray calico was fastened at the throat most primly by an oval brooch. She was sad-faced, and gray-haired, and as the German woman babbled to her, she turned and smiled upon Barbara gravely and kindly, and asked them to come in. But the German was not for sitting in a house on such a morning. The lady put on a wide hat, and gloves, and came out to the border. In her foreign language, which was merely New England English, she discussed her loves, pointing out one blossom and another. Her pansies never equaled the German's. But look at the number of buds on her peonies! She could hardly wait till they opened. And Mrs. McNair followed her about with the great question on her tongue, namely, where does one get these things in this country?

She was standing by a yellow rosebush when she asked that, first, and its owner, bending down, said;

"Here's a good little new one now. You may have that. Have you a place for it? Where do you live?"

"Twenty-five miles west."

The lady sighed.

"We have come for wood to build our house to-day," Barbara informed her.

"Have you been here long?"

"Long enough," said Barbara, simply. "I came in November."

The lady sighed again, and went to get her spade. She asked again if Barbara had a place for the rose. Barbara was offended at the suggestion she might not cherish that plant until death. Where can you buy them here? she asked again.

That rose, the lady explained, she had brought with her from Davenport, in a little box with grape cuttings and the peony, which she had carried in her lap in a covered wagon long before there were railroads to the town. She had brought it to Davenport coming down the Ohio and up the Mississippi soon after she was married. A woman had given it to her when she left Ohio for the West. The peony her mother had brought from eastern to western Ohio many years ago, and when she had died, her daughter had chosen the peony for her share of the estate. Her mother had got it from her mother, who came a bride to Ohio from western New York, clasping it against her noisy heart, out of the way of the high waters her husband had led her horse through, across unbridged streams, cherishing it more resolutely than the household stuffs which had to be abandoned in pathless woods. Her great-grandfather had brought it west in New York in his saddle bag, soon after Washington's inauguration as he returned from New York City. She supposed before that the Dutch had maybe brought it from Holland to Long Island. There had been tulips, too, but the pigs had eaten them in Ohio. She had wondered sometimes if it was the fate of the peony to be carried clear to the Pacific by lonely women. At least, if she gave a bit of it to Mrs. McNair, it would be that much farther west on its way to its destination, which she, for one, hoped it might soon reach, so that there would be some rest for women. Let Mrs. McNair remember to come for a root of it in the fall, when her fence would be finished. Without fences it is useless to try to protect flowers. Her mother in Ohio had had a sort of high stockade made of thorny brush around a little garden, so that one had to come near, and look down over the top to get a glimpse of the blossoms. But the pigs had been very hungry in those days. Their destruction of that garden and the rescue of the peony she had heard her mother tell about with tears in her eyes twenty years afterwards. It was one of the sorrows of her life.

When Mrs. McNair went home that day, she had with her the roots of all transplantable things, lilacs, white and purple, roses pink and red and yellow, pinks and young hollyhocks, grape cuttings and snowballs. She had a pile of old "Horticultural Advisers" from the lady's library, full of advice about planting windbreaks, and letters from frontier gardeners who had morning-glories growing over their young pines, and walls of hollyhocks twelve feet high. She had been urged to stay at the lady's for dinner, and the German had made her promise always to come back to her for coffee when she came to town. The road was full of ruts and swamps, and her bones ached long before the springless wagon got home. But her plants had felt no joltings, for she had held them carefully in her lap. That was the first day she sang in the United States of America. It was her "Americanization." Her husband never even noticed her song, however. He was suffering acutely from the price of glass windows.

CHAPTER XIII

Wully and Chirstie and their bonny wee Johnnie moved into their new house towards the first of May, and at the end of that month, Wully's brother John, having finished his second year in the snug little New England college, came to work for him. That institution was only fifty miles away, a distance that a lame McLaughlin, unfit for the army, walked to vote for Lincoln in sixty-four, not being able to give one great big valuable dollar for the hire of a horse. John himself walked when his sister Mary's company didn't necessitate a wagon. Having John at Wully's suited the whole family. His mother liked it because Wully was such an excellent example of patience and goodness for John, who needed just that. Chirstie liked it not only because she was spared the unpleasantness of having a strange hired man at the table, but because she saw in John the first of a succession of younger brothers, to whom, as they worked for Wully, she might in some degree repay their mother's kindness to her. Wully heartily admired John, and never neglected to point out the signs of his brilliancy to those who were interested, especially his mother. There was no one like John in the family, and therefore, of course, in the community, in Wully's estimation. The books which the other children in the little school studied ragged, John glanced at, and mastered. He never had anything to read, because the few books that Wully went slowly through, he read in an hour or two, getting more out of them in that fashion than Wully could in his. He had read every printed thing in the neighborhood: the books Wully had sent home from St. Louis, most of Scott, and some of Dickens, and Macaulay's histories. ("You understand that no stolen book comes into my house, Wully!" his mother had written him, enraged by the boys' stories of war plunder.) He had read those three hundred pious volumes that the governor of an eastern state had sent to the library of a Sunday school near by, in which he had become, in so romantic a manner, interested. He had read the college library from start to finish, and the more precious books his interested teachers would lend him. His teachers thought sometimes that John was to have a great career. But they were all amateurs in expectations, compared to his mother.

John had two very good reasons for wanting to work for Wully. The first was that at Wully's he could study all the Sabbath day in peace, which he was not allowed to do at his father's. To be sure, he was still expected to appear at church, which he did but seldom, and then only with great groans and complainings. Wully told him it wouldn't hurt him to rest his mind an hour or two once a week, and he retorted that after a week in the field, rest was the thing his mind needed least. He scolded about his father's intolerance. Wully only grinned at him, and remarked that he couldn't see that the father was much more intolerant than the son. However, if John was seized with a pain on the morning of the Sabbath, Wully wouldn't minimize his agony when his father inquired about it.

The other reason that John liked being with his brother was that there he could be sure of being paid. The summer before he had hired out to a Yankee at Fisher's Grove, for twelve dollars a month, payable in gold. He had endured food inexcusably bad, even for those circumstances, and when he had asked for his wages the man had given him, shamefacedly enough to be sure, instead of gold, one hundred and twenty acres of land! John had been barely seventeen at the time and it was years before he acknowledged that in his disappointment he had gone to the woods and cried bitterly. He could afford to tell that story with amusement when there was a town of forty thousand on that land, and he still owned most of it. That year his father had with much difficulty got a deed to the land, and mortgaged it for a little to help with the boy's schooling. He and his sister, living together on cornmeal carried from home, and working for their room rent for the kindly New Englanders with whom they lived, needed, fortunately, only a little cash. But this next year John was going to Chicago to study law. That was what the teachers advised and that would take real money.

It was one of those interested teachers who unknowingly changed the order of worship at Wully's that season. One morning, when breakfast was over at dawn, John's first week there, as Wully reached for The Book, he said in a voice which seemed, as usual, a little impatient, somewhat too eager;

"Let me do the reading, Wully, and you do the praying!"

Wully was rather surprised by such devotion on John's part.

"All right," he said, handing him the book.

John began abruptly at the first of Isaiah, which was not the place according to the custom of their fathers, and he read stumblingly, with pauses, so that his brother, turning toward him, saw that he was looking at the text only for occasional phrases, trying to read from memory. And when they sat around the table again, in the evening, almost stupid from weariness, John went over the same chapter, but with scarcely any hesitation. Wully asked him, after prayers, why he had repeated it. John had just picked up the lamp to go up to bed—he had the one lamp, because he studied—and he turned at the bottom of the stairs to answer, the light flickering across his neck, where his hickory shirt collar was open. He was six feet, even then, and he had huge broad shoulders strangely awkward. His head was long and narrow, and though he was blistered red just then from the sun, his untanned forehead was a clear yellow, unlike any other complexion in the family. He had the long upper lip that spoiled the symmetry of so many McLaughlin faces, and a long determined chin, and from his deep-set blue eyes he stood gazing at his brother with that speculating keenness with which he examined even the most familiar things.

"Professor Jamison advised me to learn Isaiah this summer. He said it would be a good thing to get the swing of the sentences. We might as well get some good out of worship, I suppose."

"Commit Isaiah to memory!" gasped Wully.

"Well, why not? We know most of it now, don't we? We've heard it all our lives. I told him we knew the Psalms. We'll read a chapter twice a day, and we'll know it."

"I won't," said Wully.

"You'll know enough of it," said John, starting up to his reading.

Wully gave Chirstie a significant look.

"Did ever you hear the equal of that?" he asked her. "I wouldn't know that chapter if I read it every day for a month." He considered John. It would not have been his father's way to use the few minutes of the day set apart for the worship of the Most High God, to learn the swing of sentences, whatever that might be. It certainly would not have been Wully's own way. But it was John's way, and doubtless a good way, and since John was living with them, he might as well have his way. Chirstie didn't mind. She only wanted John to be happy.

They were happy as the summer wore on, the three of them working from the first streak of dawn to the frog-croaking darkness. The stars in their courses and the clouds in their flights seemed to be working with them that season. Week after week, just as the ground grew ready for it, they watched the desired clouds roll up in great hills against the sky, and pour down long, slow, soaking rains. They watched the sun grow more and more stimulatingly warm, and then, just when their corn needed it, grow fiercely hot in its coaxing. They worked like slaves, of course. But then, they had always worked like slaves. Wully was at the height of his strength that year, apparently, and he tried to save John, who was, after all, still a growing boy. But John sharply refused to be considered less than any man. Chirstie was cruelly tired every night, with far too much fever. She had her new house to keep as clean as her mother's linen-hung cabin had been. She had more than a hundred little chickens to feed and water, and to guard from the slow-rising storms, and the low-hovering hawks. She had an orphan lamb to feed. She had washing to do, and ironing, and scrubbing and sewing and cooking, bread making and butter making, with pans and pails and churns to be scalded and kept sweet; she had yarn making, and knitting, vegetable drying and wild fruit canning. She had wee Johnnie to care for, and whenever she sat down to nurse him, she fell asleep worn out. More than one pie got itself scorched that way that summer.

And with it all, they were so happy that sometimes she had to say to Wully, although he didn't want her to mention it, "Oh, think of last summer, and of this!" And he would answer, "I certainly had a time without you, Chirstie!" Everything seemed to swell the sum of their well-being. Every noon, if the dinner was not entirely ready when Wully was washed for it, he seized his spade and transplanted two or three little trees from their seed-bed to their place in the windbreak. Every evening, tired to death, with the baby in his arms, he went with his wife to see if by chance any seedlings had halted, and needed water. Every leaf on the little trees called for comment. There they would stand, looking over their domain, brushing mosquitoes from their faces. Wheat and corn had surely never grown better than theirs did that year. To John, now, a field of wheat was a field of wheat, capable of being sold for so many dollars. To Wully, as to his father, there was first always, to be sure, the promise of money in growing grain, and he needed money. But besides that, there was more in it than perhaps anyone can say—certainly more than he ever said—all that keeps farm-minded men farming. It was the perfect symbol of rewarded, lavished labor, of requited love and care, of creating power, of wifely faithfulness, of the flower and fruit of life, its beauty, its ecstasy. Wully was too essentially a farmer ever to try to express his deep satisfaction in words. But when he saw his own wheat strong and green, swaying in the breezes, flushed with just the first signs of ripening, the sight made him begin whistling. And when, working to exhaustion, he saw row after row of corn, hoed by his own hands, standing forth unchoked by weeds, free to eat and grow like happy children, even though he was too tired to walk erectly, something within him—maybe his heart—danced with joy. Therefore he was then, as almost always, to be reckoned among the fortunate of the earth, one of those who know ungrudged contented exhaustion.

CHAPTER XIV

John came out for a three months' vacation the next year and worked again for Wully. They had acres of sod corn that summer, and wheat to make a miser chuckle. Both men, and whatever neighborly passer-by they might be able to hire, worked day after day till they staggered. To have stopped while yet there was sufficient daylight to distinguish another hill of corn would have been shirking; to go to supper while yet one could straighten up without a sharp pain in his back would have been laziness. Yet John was never too tired to choose an idiom as far removed as possible from the one he heard about him. Now that he had been in Chicago he had a growing contempt, which never failed to amuse Wully, for the speech of his own people. What was it they spoke, he demanded scornfully, swinging a violent hoe among the weeds. It was Scotch no longer. It wasn't English. It wasn't American, certainly. It was just a kind of—he tried all summer to describe it satisfactorily in a word. Once he called it "the gruntings of the inarticulate forthright." Mrs. Alex McNair was the only one that spoke pure anything, he declared. John seemed to like that woman, strange to say. Wully suspected he listened to her because her pronunciation fascinated him, but at Wully's he was intolerant of any tendency towards Scotticisms. Wully's and Chirstie's articulation he supervised continually, their grammar and their diction. They were not allowed to say before John, "She won't can some," or "I used to could." A less happy man than Wully might have resented correction from a younger brother. Wully took it gratefully, feeling he was getting not a poor substitute for the schooling he had been forced to miss. And when he saw his mother, he would repeat John's innovations to her with gusto. "Indeed!" she exclaimed upon one such occasion. "The gruntings of the inar—what, Wully? Lawsie me! You did well to remember that!" "Yes," cried Wully. "But John didn't remember them, mother. He makes them up!" Chirstie would have been annoyed sometimes by John's attitude, if her son had not been so devoted to his uncle. Wee Johnnie refused to go to sleep in the evening till he had had his daily romp with John on the doorstep. And even if he did treat her like an unimportant younger sister, she had to like her baby's playmate.

The child was by this time the joyous little husky heart of the family. John had noticed him dutifully at first because he was Wully's, but he came speedily to love him for his own diverting charms. There had been an evening nearly two years ago, when he came into the little room where he and his sister cooked their meals, and had found her stretched out on the bed crying. He read the letter she gave him in explanation. His mother had written about the impending disgraceful baby. John hadn't forgotten his sensation of amazement, or the sharp wound that his disdainful sense of superiority sustained, but now he seldom recalled either. It outraged his sense of the fitness of things that he so well understood that scrape; that he had to wonder at times that passion was ever less rampant, less controlled, than in the case he had to consider. The information encouraged a budding cynicism within him. If it had been anyone but Wully—even Allen—he would have understood it better. He had read the letter, and stood looking at it. Then without a word he went out, and walked about the streets through the dusk. And never a mention of it passed between the brother and sister. And then when he came home, and saw Wully—when that brotherly, honest geniality shone out simply towards him—he couldn't think of that story. Wully's presence denied it, obliterated it. That was all. And wee Johnnie justified himself.

John was, of course, keen about having his nephew speak English undefiled, and between their little games he begged him patiently to say "Uncle John." But, after hours of slipping gleefully away from effort, the baby came no nearer the desired sounds than "Diddle!" He had lovely, twinkling ways of making light of instruction. He would duck his curly head, and hold it reflectingly to one side, and purse up his little lips enough to have spoken volumes. Yet when he saw his uncle coming towards the house, he would sing out that absurd "Diddle," delightedly, waiting an award for such perfect enunciation. When his grandmother got him into her arms, she would beg him to say "Grannie." And he would say it, in a way that satisfied him entirely. Only he called the word "Pooh!" And in that absurdity, too, he persisted. "Mama" he said, and "Papa" and "chickie" and "Diddle" and "Pooh." And that was all. No coaxing could elicit more from him. Chirstie grew vexed at times hearing other women tell how early and plainly their children had talked. She longed to have Johnnie shine vocally. Sometimes she almost wondered if he wasn't "simple." But her mother-in-law consoled her by telling about her John. He had spoken hardly a word till he was three, and she was really getting alarmed about it, when suddenly he seemed to join the family conversation, so rapidly he learned words and sentences.

So with that foolish "Ayn?" which was his question, and with the "Ayn" which was his consent, Bonnie Wee Johnnie went on ruling his domain. The men never started to the fields with a team without letting the baby ride a few steps on the back of the old mare. No one plowed into a bird's nest without saving an egg to show the baby. No one ran across a long gaudy pheasant's feather without saving it for Johnnie's soft fingers to feel. At noon John carried him out to pat the colt's nose, or to see the little pigs nosing their way among one another to their mother's milk. The baby had just naturally become Wully's child. Wully could never bear the thought of Peter Keith. He kept it resolutely out of his mind. He had to. He shrank from it as he had never shrunk from the face of an enemy. Making the baby his own helped the forgetting. Barbara McNair said to Isobel McLaughlin that she had never seen a man with such a way with a baby as Wully had with that child. And Isobel McLaughlin answered that it was small wonder Wully had a way with babies, since he had carried one in his arms ever since he was three years old. Month by month Wully became in the eyes of that prairie-bound world a more exemplary and unsuspected father to Chirstie's son.

June came and went. The corn began hiding the black soil at its roots entirely from sight. It was "knee-high by the Fourth of July" according to the Scriptures. There was to be a great celebration that year in Woolsey's woods, and Wully had, of course, planned to take his family to the picnic. All his army comrades would be there, and neighbors for thirty miles round, talking crops and prices, and the president's troubles in Washington. It was to have been a grateful change from hoeing.

However, when the day came, it was out of the question to take Chirstie, who had been having fever, and the baby, who was unhappily teething, for a twenty-five mile ride through the heat, even with the new spring seat which Wully had bought for the wagon—extravagantly, according to Alex McNair. John, therefore, rode away on horseback before dawn. Not that John would have condescended to care to go if it had been only what he would have called in our day a gathering of "neighborhood fatheads." But there was to be a speaker there who helped to make laws and thwart the president in Washington, and John wanted to hear what he had to say, and how he managed to say it.

Wully and Chirstie accordingly began their holiday by a most unusually long sleep in the morning, the baby for some reason allowing it. They had a late and lazy breakfast. If Chirstie cared to, they would drive down to the creek and look for some blackberries, Wully said. He dallied about, playing with the baby, who was better than they had expected him to be. They sauntered out to their garden of little trees, after Wully had wiped the breakfast dishes, and spent some time there, weeding it, and cultivating it, playing together. Were not the two of them quite content to spend their holiday at home together now? It was not as if they were young, unmated things, running about experimentally, investigatingly. When it grew warm, and they sought the shade of the house to rest in, a Sabbath peace brooded over them. Wully stretched out on the grass, and the baby sat contentedly on his chest.

Chirstie looked at the morning-glories blooming on the fence of the little vegetable garden. There were but few of them. The hens had got into the garden earlier and scratched them almost all out. She hated to kill the hens she had had the trouble of raising, just because they spoiled her morning-glories. Her stepmother, she reflected, had no such hesitations. If a rash hen flew into Barbara McNair's garden, she caught it and cut its wing feathers. If it repeated the offense, into the boiling kettle it went. She had scarcely a hen left. That famous wee white fowl-house was really little more than an ornament. Yet when Chirstie sighed over her morning-glories, Wully said at once that he would get a better fence around a bigger garden by the next spring. He, too, was thinking of the McNair place. Everyone thought of that place that summer, and planned to make his own less desolate-looking. That McNairs' was now the very show place of the country. One driving up to it, unless he had heard reports, could scarcely believe his eyes. No sty now! No bony cows trampling knee-deep in mud! One saw a trim white house, inside a smart white fence, upon a jaunty rise of ground, with a gay white fowl-house in the rear, and in the front yard—what sights for pioneer eyes! Crimson hollyhocks, just beginning to open, almost as high as the lean-to, screening the porch. A grapevine halfway across the main part of the building. Morning-glories on cunning arrangements of hidden wires. Scarlet poppies and magenta petunias romping all along the front walk, laughing to the confederate heavens, flaunting their uselessness flippantly before the eyes of those who lived slavishly, blossoms with the Scriptures behind them to justify their toiling not, their spinning not, their being arrayed beyond kings' glory—not economically. The garden scouted the very principles of the hard-working, of those who would "get ahead." It hooted aloud at frugality. Barbara McNair kept a lamb, to be sure, but for no utilitarian purpose. She kept it to mow her lawn. And when its hunger had shaved its environments, she moved the stake which held it, to another spot. She kept hens languidly, perhaps only to justify artistically that supernumerary luxury, the white fowl-house. But let those chickens beware how they turned their eyes towards her garden spaces, lest they discover fatally her feelings towards them and their like. No useless and ungardening orphan calf would she mother. No bereaved young pigs owed their life to her. She did only what she elected to do. Though there was at that time scarcely a servant girl west of the Mississippi, Barbara McNair was almost never without some neighbor girl to do her work for her, while in return she taught her sewing, or made some pretty garment for her. Just now Wully's sister Mary, who was to marry a Yankee minister that fall, was working at the McNairs', while Barbara, in spite of Isobel McLaughlin's protests, was making her a famous blue silk dress, equaled in grandeur only by that red wool one of Chirstie's. Always some girl or other eating that helpless McNair's good bread, while his wife knit tidies, and watered her trifling wee flowers—from a pump all painted and handy just outside the kitchen door—and lived like a lady, envied by all the women in the neighborhood, and distrusted by nearly all the men.

Wully lay playing with the baby, who liked tickling his face with a long spear of grass, and thinking just how he would make that fence, and grinning, at times, to himself. The Sabbath before he had taken Chirstie home for dinner, and when she had seen how the flowers were blooming there, she had explained in vexation about her morning-glories. Wully had been walking with his father-in-law and the women among the trifling flowers, when Chirstie had spoken of the accident, in answer to Barbara McNair's question. And Alex had turned to Wully, and remonstrated with him for not having a better fence for Chirstie! A man ought to see that the women had such things, McNair had assured him solemnly. That was one of the best things he had had to tell his mother for a long time! Alex McNair telling him, Wully McLaughlin, how to treat a wife! McNair strutted about, taking all the credit for that garden, extremely proud of having the best-looking place for miles around. As if he had been able to help himself! Wully had said nothing about the incident to Chirstie. He couldn't seem always to be laughing at her father. Just then she went on to tell him about the new dress Barbara had made for little Jeannie. Whatever the neighbors might say enviously about Barbara McNair, they must in justice agree that she was an excellent stepmother to her husband's children. The way she loved Jeannie and Dod, and was loved in return, was a source of deep satisfaction to Chirstie. And so she gossiped contentedly and harmlessly on about the neighbors, and the baby kicked the protesting Wully gleefully in the ribs. They felt cosily shut in to themselves by the sense of the countryside emptied of its patriotic and picnicking dwellers. Wully lounged about till almost eleven. There was a little hay cut which he wanted to turn. He would be back by dinner time, he said.

He started down the path to the hayfield, taking the scythe with him. It was a hot day, but there was a lively breeze blowing the grass into waves and billows, and momentary disappearing swift maelstroms. Safe white clouds were sailing on high, but along the horizon hints of much rain were gathering slowly. It wouldn't be safe to cut much hay in face of them. He really need not have brought the scythe. He began turning what was cut, forkful by forkful. Then he cut a few swathes. Working, he lay bare a marsh hawk's nest. He stopped for breath, and stood watching the catlike birdlings turn on their backs and offer fight with their pawing, scrawny claws, while the mother circled angrily about him. He must tell Chirstie about those warlike babies. He went on, to leave them in peace. He kept getting farther and farther away from the house, towards the far edge of the plot of prairie they had chosen for hay. He worked away, scarcely lifting his head from his task, wondering occasionally if the rain, undoubtedly gathering, would come by night.

Suddenly he heard a cry. He looked up. He threw down his scythe. He started running. Chirstie was running towards him. She was crying out to him, too far away to be heard. He gave a look towards the house. There seemed to be no sign of fire. He tore on towards her. It must be the baby. He saved his breath till he got near her. She stumbled against him, gasping, fainting. What she managed to say brought the contentment of his life crashing down to ruin.

"It's Peter! Peter Keith! He's back!"

She would have fallen. He caught her. He held her against him. She couldn't speak. He couldn't believe his ears.

"You said he wouldn't come back!" she began, again. "Wully, he took hold of me! He—" She Was weeping with rage and terror. "Look here!" Her sleeve was torn half off. "You said he wouldn't come back!" she cried, shaking.

"You're dreaming!" he cried. He couldn't believe it. It wasn't possible.

"He came to the door," she sobbed. "I didn't see him till then. I'm not dreaming! Look at my dress! Where you going? Don't leave me alone!"

He had started for his gun. Rage came over him like a fever mounting. The sight of that torn sleeve made him suddenly blind with anger. He couldn't believe it. It wasn't possible that man had dared to come back and lay violent hands on his wife. It simply couldn't be. She was calling to him to wait for her. She wouldn't be left alone.

He helped her along blindly. He had never known such murderous anger. He wanted her to hurry. He lusted for that gun. He felt her trembling against him. By God, his wife wouldn't have to tremble much longer!

It seemed to him long before they came to their house—very long. "Don't you let him hurt you!" she moaned as they came up to it. He strode into the kitchen. There the baby slept in his cradle, and flies walked leisurely over the piecrust scattered over the floor. He seized his gun. He went to the east door, and looked out. He went to the west door. He stood looking. Before his eyes hens scratched for their broods in peace. He searched the house. He turned to go to the barn. She cried after him, "Oh, don't let him hurt you!" He went without caution, madly. But in the barn there was no enemy. No sign of a man behind the barn, where the grass billows chased one another. No one hiding about the haystack. He strode about seeking. There was no enemy in any place. But beyond the little tree bed, and the garden, beyond the wheat fields—what might be there, to the east to the west, to the north and the south, in those wild man-high grasses! There a thousand men might hide and laugh at pursuers. Looking at those baffling stretches, Wully choked. He was helpless.

He went back to his wife. She was trying vainly to compose herself. "I never thought he would come! I never imagined it! You said he wouldn't, Wully!" Didn't she see how that reproach must madden him! "I was just standing there, making the pie. He came to that door. I thought it was you. And when I looked up, he was looking at me, Wully!" She wailed out that last. "He was looking at me. I didn't know what to do. He just grabbed me!" She buried her face in her arms, and sobbed.

God! If only he could get hold of that snake who hid in the grasses! He turned abruptly again to the search.

"Stay with me!" she cried. "Where you going?"

"There's no one here," he answered, beside himself, wanting to comfort her. "Come and see for yourself!" Trembling and crying she came out with him to the barn. That morning there was no great cement-floored barn to search through, in whose loft a hundred men might lie, nor long feeding sheds for steers, nor any tower-like silos. There were no scattered groups of lighted hog-houses, nor garages nor heated drinking tanks. There were no machine sheds, nor ventilated corn-cribs, nor power plants nor icehouses, as now there are. Only that one little unconcealing barn, those small slight plantings, that innocent wheat, that shaved patch of the prairie which was the hayfield.

"He's run out there!" Chirstie moaned, pointing to the distances. Somewhere out there he had lain in wait, perhaps, seeing Wully depart, maybe watching their just caresses. Somewhere out there he must be pausing now, watching them hunt for him. Wully was shaking with incredulous fury. It simply wasn't possible that Peter Keith should so have underestimated him! But no wonder, after he had been such a fool as to let him go unpunished once! Oh, all Wully needed was one more chance at him....

They ate no dinner. Chirstie lay down wearily. Wully with his gun in hand, stood watching, promising her he wouldn't go far, or leave her alone more than a minute. She moaned as he came to her during the afternoon, to give her the baby;

"Oh, what'll we ever do now, Wully!"

"Leave that to me!" he said, in such a voice that she could say no more just then.

"You won't hurt him, Wully!" she begged again, thinking only of her husband's safety.

"Will I not!" he answered grimly. She wept.

"There's Aunt Libby!" she moaned.

"Is there!" he cried. There was no auntie in his intentions. He was thinking only of his wife—who trembled and wept, temporarily.

"Wully, you'll get into trouble! If he won't bother us, let him come back!"

"He does bother me!" She dared not answer that tone. Wully choked, and turned away, to look out over the prairies again. A rattlesnake, that man was, hiding in the grass, a damned poison snake, and like a snake he should be treated. If it had been a windless day, one might have traced him through the grasses. But now one second of the wind swept away any trace of him. A good dog might have trailed him. But there was no dog at hand. In many places before Wully's very eyes, a man—a snake—might walk upright and unperceived. Inside, Chirstie lay moaning in fever. Outside, Wully patrolled his premises, frustrated, raging.

In his excitement details came rushing back to his mind to which he had long and obstinately refused entrance. He remembered all the bits of confession that Chirstie had made to him the first night that, knowing her trouble, he had gone to claim her. Peter had loved her, he had wanted her for his, she had told him. But she wouldn't listen to him, because she thought of Wully. She thought of herself as his. That was when she was living at her aunt's, after her mother had died. Then once Aunt Libby had gone to stay with her sister who was having a baby. Wully could curse that woman's name for having so blindly, so fondly, trusted her knavish son. Why couldn't she have at least left Dod with his sister! But Chirstie hadn't been afraid. Wasn't Peter her cousin? She hadn't been at all afraid. And that night, when there was no help within a mile, she had run out of the house, undressed, barefooted, across the snow—till Peter caught her, and brought her back. Wully hadn't often thought of that, because he couldn't think of it and live. But it had no mercy on him now. That story cried aloud to him, shrieking through his mind. He would kill that man, and go to the sheriff and give himself up. He would stand up and tell any twelve men in the county that story, and come home acquitted. If only he could find the man! He went beating through the grasses nearer him, maddened by the feeling that it was in vain. To the west the treacherous grasses jeered at him wavingly, and to the east. North and south they mocked him.

The afternoon passed. Neither of them could eat at supper time. Chirstie wouldn't stay alone in the house while he went to milk. She insisted on crawling out to the barn, to be near him. She could scarcely sit up, so worn and weak she was. The baby howled bitterly, being neglected. Wully put him to sleep, laying him on the bed beside his mother. He shut the door to the east. It had no lock. It had never needed one. He put a chair against it, and sat down on the step of the other door, fingering his gun as the stars came out, watching, thinking sorely.

There was no jury that would not set him free when he told the story. What sort of men would those be who would say he had not done right to kill a poison snake? He would just tell them—ah, but to tell that story, now, when it was being so well forgotten! To bring it all back to sneering ears, as it had been brought back to him so painfully fresh to-day! If only he could find the man, and kill him quietly, and bury him somewhere in the tall grasses, without anyone knowing! If only he might find him crouching there somewhere! So desirable did that consummation seem that he turned abruptly and went to the barn, to see if his spade, which his father had borrowed, had been returned to its place. Yes, there it was. He could laugh as he dug that grave in the farthest, most remote slough! By God, only two years ago the government of the United States had been paying him for digging graves, graves for honest men, who made no women tremble. Oh, if he might find that man, and get it over quietly! That wish became a drunken cursing prayer in his mind. If only in the morning he might only say to her, "You needn't be afraid he will ever come back again!"

Terrible things rushed through his mind. Once when the baby had been a few days old, he had asked her a question curiously, casually. She had seemed so surprised in those days that she hadn't had twins. He had asked her why she had supposed she would, and when she had not answered, he had asked her again. She said simply that after all that had happened that night, she thought she couldn't have less. He had really so successfully pretended to make light of her situation that she didn't know how that must rankle in his mind. He had turned and gone abruptly out into the darkness, when she had answered him so, and she never realized what she had done. He had wondered then why he had ever let that man go.

He had wondered often at the time of the child's birth. Well, once he got a chance now, he would be done with that regret forever....

He remained on guard, not realizing how the hours were passing, till he heard John riding hurriedly in home. He went to look at the clock then. It was midnight. The storm was almost upon them. The thunder was growling about its coming.

John sat down on the step, and Wully sat down near him, intending not to let John know what had happened. The speaker, John began, had been traveling through the South, and strange things he had seen. He said Johnson ought to be impeached. Wully had a vague idea what his brother was saying. He didn't want to excite his suspicion in the least. He rallied, and asked if Stowe had been there. John had seen Stowe, and Stowe had asked why Wully wasn't there. Lots of friends had asked about Wully. John talked on. The thunder grew louder. Rain began falling, in big drops. They both rose to go in. Rising, John said;

"Yes! And as I was coming home, guess whom I met, Wully! Our esteemed kinsman, Peter Keith! I stopped in at O'Brien's, and there he was, drinking away as usual. Wasn't that interesting, now, for us? And Aunt Libby was going about all day as usual, asking if anyone had seen her poor, sick blessed laddie. I brought him as far home as the McTaggerts' corner. Maybe auntie will lapse into sanity now, comparative sanity, at least!"

Wully had risen with John, to follow him into the house, but at the sound of that name he had paused outside the door, to hide his face from his brother. John's story made him heartsick. There seemed no chance now of getting it over secretly. Peter had gone home! It didn't seem possible. He intended to defy Wully! He intended to hide behind his mother. Well, he would speedily find that no woman's skirts could save him now from his deserts. He feigned a natural interest, and tarried outside till he heard John going up the stairs. Then he came in from the rain, and sat down. That room, that home of theirs, all spoiled, all defiled. Their table, their chairs, their clock, all the things that they had bought and enjoyed together, seemed alien and sinister. He gave a look around all the little room wonderingly, and then it all faded from his thought. He laid his arms on the table, and buried his face in them, as if he was weeping. But he was not weeping. Until almost morning he sat that way, scarcely moving, not heeding the sharp breaking of the thunder. He was planning ghastly things. Chirstie called to him sometimes, and he answered. She called to him at length wearily to come to bed.

To take his place beside her! Oh, God!

She was his wife, and he hadn't been able to defend her! But morning was coming. The new day's light would make things right.

CHAPTER XV

"You go on with the corn," Wully said to John at breakfast. "I'm taking Chirstie over to mother's." John made no comment. Chirstie looked as if she had had fever unusually severe the day before, and naturally she would be better cared for at the McLaughlins'. John suspected nothing. He wasn't especially observant. Talking still of the celebration, he didn't see Wully watching his wife, covertly watching the way her eyes turned hauntedly toward any slight sound out of doors. Wully went through with the prayers as usual. "Prosper us in our duties this day!" he implored, with unaccustomed fervency. John went away to his work. Chirstie and the baby got into the wagon, where Wully had slyly hidden his gun—he had to conceal his sterner purpose from her. He said to her simply that he had made Peter get out once, and he could do it again. He saw no use in saying how much more thoroughly he intended doing it this time.

They scarcely spoke, riding away together, man and wife. Sitting there, so close to him, she seemed so dear ... so dear ... and life so precious.... Why should he have to endanger it now just when he was beginning to appreciate it, for the sake of that man's villainy! The poignant silence struggled and surged about them, his rage, her fear, their love fighting together with no relief in expression, her beseeching, warning eyes searching the face he tried to keep averted.

No one at his mother's had heard of Peter's return. That was proved by the fact that no one began talking about it. Chirstie had had fever the day before, Wully announced to them shortly. He was worried about her. He had to go over to the store, and he thought she had better be left where she could have some care. He said he and John could "bach it" a few days. She spoke up sharply and demanded that he come for her by evening at least. He had to promise that much, to keep her from exciting suspicion. It was plain she meant to take no denial. Her eyes implored him to be careful.

Lightened of his encumbrances, he drove away. He was praying that circumstances might be made to serve him, so that he could get his task over secretly. If not, then Peter would find that no woman could help him now! He drove straight along towards his aunt's, grimly, not having to nurse his wrath, having only to restrain it. He wasn't made for anger, as he knew. It had even as a little boy always made him ill. It had exhausted him now. He felt limp. And he must be strong and calm for what was coming. He let his horses take their own gait. The heat of the sun, after the rain of the night, was making the country one great steam bath. He wiped the sweat from his forehead.

He came to the McTaggerts' corner. John had seen that man so far home the night before. If John had known then all that story, what a chance he would have had. Thank God he hadn't known! But when he did know, to-day, now, in a few hours, he would stand by Wully with what a sincere strength! Of course John couldn't be expected to stay and look after the farm while Wully was taken—where? Maybe Andy would do that. And Chirstie would have to stay at his mother's until—what? His happiness was scarcely more now than a sickening faint memory. He could do what he had to do. The McLaughlins could always do that. And do it well!

He could see the little Keith house now. He drove on towards it. There was no one working in the hayfield. There was no one hoeing corn. No sign of life but a tethered colt in the path. He drove up, and got out of the wagon. He tied his steaming horses to the barn. He hadn't taken his gun into his hands yet, when the door opened, and his aunt came out.

She was ready for some work in the garden apparently. She wore a kind of sunbonnet made by sewing a ruffle of old calico part way round a man's old cap, to protect her neck from the sun. She saw Wully, and her face lightened with a greeting.

"Is it you, Wully!" she exclaimed. "And how's Chirstie the day? We missed you yesterday. She had too much fever, I doubt—"

"She's better. She's at mother's. Where's everybody?"

"Your uncle's at the McNairs'."

Trying to hide that skunk, was she!

"I want to see Peter!"

"What Peter?" she asked with a start.

"Your Peter!"

"My Peter!"

"Yes!" She needn't think she could work that!

"Did you think he was here, Wully?" she asked, hurt.

"John saw him last night," he cried accusingly.

"What John?"

"Our John! He saw him last night!"

"Saw who?"

"Saw your Peter!" Could it be—

"Saw my Peter!"

"He came home with him last night as far as the McTaggerts'!"

"Last night!"

"Yes!"

"With my Peter!"

"Yes!" stammered Wully.

Peter had never got home. There was no doubt about that.

Libby Keith was standing transfixed there. Her gray face began working.

Suddenly she put her hand up to her head, and gave a moan.

"He's destroyed! He never got to me!"

She started and ran past Wully in the path, and had climbed into his wagon before he could stop her. She gave his hitched horses such a slap with the lines that they plunged strongly. He sprang to get them before they broke away. He jumped to his place and seized the lines.

"You can't go with me!" he shouted at her. He couldn't throw her out of the wagon, and the horses were all he could manage, thanks to her excitement. As if in obedience to the thoughts of the humans behind them, they were racing down the path towards the McCreaths', over which Wully had just come.

"You can't come with me!" he cried again.

She never heeded him.

"He'll have stopped at the McCreaths'!" she said, moaning. Moaning ... and making little sounds of speed to his team, which couldn't possibly have been tearing ahead more madly. She sat rocking back and forth, and making sounds which unmanned him, overwrought as he was by his own excitement and hatred. Through the steaming slough they plunged and splashed. He didn't care now how quickly they came to their destination. He gave up trying to control the horses. Anything to get away from that noise she was making, that anguished crooning. Never was a man with murder in his heart so undone by the grief he intended augmenting.

The sandy-haired bewhiskered McCreath had stopped still in his dooryard to watch the runaway team coming up. When he saw who it was, he dropped the hoe in his hand, and came on out down the path to meet the evident crisis. Wully pulled up the panting horses, and before they had stopped, Libby Keith cried to the man approaching,

"Where is he? Where's my Peter?"

At first he could not understand so impossible a question. She scrambled perilously down, and started on a run for the house, with him following.

"Where is he?" she cried again, turning on him. Then McCreath understood. She was mad, the poor body. He said gently;

"He isn't here, you know, Libby. Peter isn't here."

"He is!" she cried. "He's come! They seen him!"

Wully had followed them. McCreath turned to him, and got a nod in confirmation. They were at the door, now, and Mrs. McCreath had come that far to see what the disturbance was. McCreath cried heartily to his wife;

"Peter's home, Aggie!"

Tears sprang quickly to Aggie's eyes.

"Where is he!" Libby cried at the same moment.

"He's not here, you know," McCreath repeated kindly.

"Not here!" Libby repeated.

"John saw him last night," Wully cried angrily.

"Where?" they all demanded.

John had seen him at O'Brien's, and as far on the way home as the McTaggerts' corner. And they had supposed he must have turned in at the McCreaths' when the storm came up.

"He's at the McTaggerts', then!" McCreath seemed sure of it. But Libby Keith couldn't wait till the words were out of his mouth. She was down the path again, and climbing up into the wagon, and the McCreaths were following her, breathing out their congratulations. They didn't know when any news had pleased them as much as that. They were that glad for her. They were shouting after the galloping team in vain.

And again he had to sit by her, as she went on again, crooning and whimpering, making noises like a shot rabbit. He would drive his horses till they fell in their tracks to get away from that torture.

On the corner, where the little path from the Keiths' joined the wider road, the McTaggerts were building a house. Three men were working on the roof of it, and from the vantage of the height they watched the team flying towards them. They speculated about it. They came down.

"Where's my Peter?" she shouted to them before they could hear her. She kept shouting it as she climbed down.

They stared at her.

They hadn't seen anything of her Peter.

They had to go all over that again. John McLaughlin had seen him at this corner last night. Where was he now?

Wully wouldn't be balked. Libby Keith wouldn't be cheated. The McTaggerts stood looking at the two blankly.

Where was Jimmy McTaggert, who had been drinking with Peter last night? He ought to know.

Jimmy McTaggert was wakened from the sleep that followed his holiday spree, and dragged to the light of the morning, half clothed.

He remembered nothing. Wully turned from him wrathfully. Where was his older brother? Let Gib be brought. Gib wouldn't have been too drunk to remember. Gib was in a far field. A boy went for him horseback. They made Libby sit down. They stood around dazed. Wully went on explaining what he knew again and again. It seemed hours before Gib appeared.

There stood Gib before them, telling the truth, and making it believed. They had come with John from O'Brien's to be sure, and at the corner John had ridden on home, and Peter had turned and gone walking down the path towards home. That was all that Gib knew about it. Peter had walked right along, not staggering, or seeming drunk.

The men stood looking blankly at one another, fumbling among possibilities, in quietness—for one second.

Then Libby cried out.

"He's fallen! He's destroyed!" She started down the path, towards the road calling him, making a more terrible sound than ever—a stronger sound.

"Lammie!" she cried. "Where are you? Mother's coming!" Some place between that corner and her home she thought him lying helpless, dying maybe. Lying drunk, the men thought, and nodded significantly to each other. It flashed through Wully's bewildered mind that he had probably started back towards Chirstie. Or maybe back to O'Brien's, someone suggested. Mrs. McTaggert was running after Libby Keith. The men started to help her search. In decency they could do no less. They tried to soothe her. He would be sleeping somewhere. Had she looked in her own barn? Could it be, they wondered vaguely, thinking of her other children, that had happened ... anything tragic?

Wully had to join them. After all, she was mad, stark mad and shrieking over the prairies, and she wasn't a McTaggert that they should have to care for her. She was his father's sister, and he must see what became of her. Down the road she ran, calling out to her son, and commanding them. They were to go for her husband. They were to get her brothers, her neighbors, to send men on horses to look for him. Some of them turned back to obey her. Wully ran along with her.

Beating along both sides of the road they went, tramping down the grasses, calling him—calling till Wully felt tears running down his face. Not that he pitied her. He cursed her. He was saying to himself, "God damn you, stop that noise!" And to her, habit-bound as he was, and shrinking from the pain of her voice, "Let me do the shouting, Auntie! Let me call for you!" He didn't know his voice when he lifted it. So how could Peter know who was begging him for an answer! Oh, if only he might come across him there, fallen, and make an end of this horror! Sometimes he stayed a distance from her in this wild hope. Sometimes he had to support her to keep her from falling. Down through the slough they went, splashing and bedraggled. Mrs. McTaggert, with a baby in her arms, followed as best she might. The slough was shallow where the path crossed it, but how deep the waters might be on either side, no one knew. Libby Keith stretched out her arms dramatically towards them.

"Lammie! Mother's coming!" she implored.

Mrs. McTaggert sobbed. But she sobbed only like a woman. Not like a ....

CHAPTER XVI

The neighborhood gathered at the alarm. By noon Wully's father and mother were at the Keiths', and the heads of families for miles around. Up and down the road the boys and younger men were halloing and beating about, and in the kitchen the wise old heads were holding a consultation. Young John McLaughlin had been sent for—that is, Wully's brother John, not the Squire's John—and all the men who according to Gib McTaggert's story must have seen Peter the night before. As the elders waited their coming, they debated solemnly. What could have happened to a man between the McTaggerts' corner and his home? A drunken man. A man said always to be weak. A man known to be lazy. With a storm coming on. And sharp lightning. A dark road, with deep waters not far from it. Blinded by the lightning could he have turned from the path and been drowned? Could he have fallen and broken a leg? Men have broken bones as they walked. Was he now lying helpless somewhere about? If he was as weak as his mother always insisted, might he not have fallen down drunk, and lying in the way throughout the night, now be overcome by fever? Could he have been bitten by a rattler, and, asleep, died of the poison? Could the lightning have struck him? Men wondered, rather than dared to ask aloud, could there have been a drunken quarrel, and blows perhaps fatal. Wully suggested that he might be in hiding, but this was considered a simple suggestion to come from him, and no one gave it any attention. They all seemed to think that it was his mother Peter was trying to get to.... Wully dared not explain what reason he might have for hiding. He wished he had not suggested such a thing.

The young men came, and submitted to questionings. None of them knew exactly when Peter had arrived at O'Brien's. There had been a fight at the saloon. Young Sproul had still a black eye from it, and after Bob McWhee had knocked him down, there had been a few bad minutes when the onlookers wondered if he was ever to rise again. It had been exciting, to say the least. And men had been busy pacifying the two. After that, Peter was there ... though no one remembered to have seen him coming in. He hadn't asked for anything to eat. He had drunken quietly, and been silent. Wully, who had been swallowing his wrath as best he might all the morning, as man after man came out of pity for Libby Keith, each man's kindness to her making Wully's purpose seem the greater sin against the mother— Wully couldn't understand this story about Peter's quietness. Peter gabbled, naturally. He went noisily on and on. And now, not a man who had seen his surprising return, could report definitely a thing he had said. He hadn't really said anything. Wully's brother John testified that when he first saw him, he asked him if he had come back to see his mother. Libby Keith, listening with her harrowed soul, saw no sarcasm in such a greeting. Peter had just mumbled something in reply. It had never occurred to John that Peter hadn't been home. He thought of course he had had supper there. It seemed strange to no one that John had desired no further intercourse with his cousin. His story agreed with that of all the others. He had tarried but a few minutes at the saloon, naturally, and besides, there was the storm coming on. He had cared enough for the family name to get Peter started on his way home with the McTaggerts. The young Jimmy McTaggert had sung Psalms obscenely all the way along, and Peter had sat on the side of the wagon. He hadn't been too drunk to hold on there over all the joltings. John had left him getting down at the corner. Then the great honest young McTaggert took up the story, and lucky indeed it was for his wildly drinking young brother that no one doubted what he had to say. Even O'Brien, the whisky-selling man whose name was anathema to mothers of rollicking sons and erring husbands, came volunteering his futile help.

They organized the search. They divided into parties. Some were to venture out into the deep waters of the more probable sloughs. Some were to hunt the woods towards O'Brien's, because Peter was always wanting another drink, and might have turned, befuddled, in that direction. Some were to hunt through the creek underbrush. Wully chose to go with one of the parties towards the creek, partly because that would take him past his father's, and he was anxious to warn Chirstie under no provocation to tell yet what she knew, and partly because in that way he would get farthest away from his aunt. He felt as if all the solid faithful earth under his feet had given way, and he was attempting to cling to—just nothing. That woman, his aunt, had harvested before him all the sympathy that should have been his. When now he had killed Peter, the community would think only of her sorrow. There would be no thought of the justification of the man constrained to his murder. There was an intense unfairness about it all, some way. Wully was consoled dumbly by the Squire's half-heartedness in the search. He grumbled as he went along about having to go. And Wully's heart warmed to him, not knowing that the Squire's sensualism, like all men's, had always to be at war with maternity, which was Libby Keith. Wully had time to question John privately, but he got no further information. Even Chirstie could explain nothing. "Did he look sick?" Wully demanded of her anxiously. "He was drunk, wasn't he?" She drew back from the question. "Oh, don't ask me!" she murmured. "He just looked—at me!"

The men spent all day in the more unfathomable menaces. The women searched back and forth about the Keiths' house. The two miles between that house and the corner, back and forth, up and down that road, they beat persistently and prayerfully, until the little path of the day before was a great river-bed of trodden muddy grass hiding nothing. They searched all impossible places; through the Keiths' and McCreaths' and McTaggerts' barns they went again and again. Peter hadn't disappeared out of existence. He was somewhere. Likely somewhere between the house and the corner. They went over that path continually till their children began to cry for supper.

The men stopped not even to eat. Let the women and the children do the chores. Let them go undone. Steaming and weary and excited, they went on with their hunt till the sun set, till the last glimmer of twilight was gone. Now none was as persevering as the Squire. The hunt had become for him the greatest game of his maturity. One by one in the darkness the men had at length to ride home to their waiting families, with no news. Strange things they had to think on, places in the swamps where they had not been able to touch bottom, places where the rushes grew rank and thick with scarcely space enough for nest of the crying waterbirds—stretches with no sign of a lost man, and no hope for one losing himself....

At the Keiths' Isobel McLaughlin in Peter's bed in the kitchen was lying praying. Except his mother, no one prayed as fervently for Peter's safe return as Isobel. All that she asked of the Almighty was that Peter might be found alive and well enough to take the shame away from her good innocent Wully. If Peter was brought home dead—how then ever, in the face of Libby's grief, could she say that the beloved was a scoundrel! How could she ever endure not saying it? That would be too bitter a dose for her. Let God not give her that cup to drink! If fervency could have brought an answer to prayer, how quickly would Peter have appeared!

Her passionate hope had been some consolation to Libby, who so little understood the reason for it. Libby was lying down in her room, not because Isobel had besought her to, but because she was no longer able to stand up. Isobel wanted to get some rest, but she couldn't leave off her praying to God, the good Father. She hoped Libby might sleep till morning.

But the moon rose after midnight, and with the first flicker of its light, Libby came out of the bedroom, tying a skirt about her. Isobel sat up in bed.

"There's moonlight now," said Libby. Even from the doorway, where she stood in the darkness, Isobel could hear her breathing.

"Lie down, Libby!" she implored.

"I mind wee Jennie Price," said Libby.

"Ah, Libby!" protested Isobel, shrinking from the mention of such poignancy. Jennie Price was the six-year-old who had been lost in the grasses, wandering from her home some twenty miles down the creek, a year or two ago. What but that had all the women been thinking of all the day and shrinking from mentioning.

Libby was groping about for her shoes which she had left in the kitchen.

"Just near home, Isobel! Forty yards from her mother's door."

"You can't go out by night, Libby. You can't stand up!"

"Crawling towards home, it may be."

"Libby! Libby!" cried Isobel, getting up. Forty yards from home they had found the girlish skeleton the next spring, in a place a hundred men would swear in court they had sought through dozens of times. The mother herself had come upon it. Had the child been stolen away for some evil purpose, and flung back later to die? No one would ever know.

"The wee bones were all white, Isobel!"

"Spare us, Libby! Peter's a man grown!"

The women went out calling down the road together. At dawn, when John McCreath came out to milk, while yet the stars were shining, he heard Libby calling hoarsely, "Lammie! Lammie! Your mother's coming!"

CHAPTER XVII

By that time men were beginning to gather again—middle-aged men on horseback, stiff from years of toil, bearded great young men with dogs at their heels, large-boned, ruddy, gaunt, rugged of face like Lincoln, overgrown boys, and boys of the very smallest size which fearful mothers could be persuaded to let go into possible danger—they came walking or riding towards the Keiths' for thirty miles away. The younger ones were sent on horseback to spread the news along all the roads towards town, even along obscure untraveled paths that led to the cross-state coach road to the north. In the morning council Wully had again ventured to suggest that Peter had of his own accord gone back to the place from which he had so mysteriously come. Again they all refused to consider his suggestion. Was it likely a man should return without a glimpse of those he had come so far to see? The whole thing was baffling. It seemed beyond belief that no one had seen him come. That could have happened only on such a day as the Fourth, when all the settlers were away from home. Wully wondered to himself, grimly, however, why, if Peter had managed to come once, unperceived, he would not be able to come again as slyly. He didn't see that to tell what he knew would ease the situation. And he had no intention of telling it if he had proof that it would have ended the search. He would tell that tale only to justify his making Chirstie safe from violence. He felt strangely distant from those whose eagerness to help increased with each glimpse they got of Libby Keith. At his father's bidding he went again with a party to search the creek underbrush.

From morning till noon they went on fighting their way through the impenetrable briary wall of green, stopping only for breath at the water's edge, scratched, mosquito-bitten, baffled, exhausted. Once John and Wully happened to get to the bank at the same moment, and John, stooping down to wash his face, said to his brother, carefully lowering his voice;

"I wouldn't be at all surprised if you are right, Wully. It would be just like Peter to have to leave some place suddenly, in some scrape. I think it probable, after all, that he had started on short notice for the west, and passing O'Brien's, was unable to resist the smell. He wouldn't even have had the decency to go to see his mother if he had been within half a mile of the house!"

Wully said nothing to this, but it comforted him to know how low John's opinion of Peter was. He could work with new energy after that. At noon the ten of them stopped at the nearest house for dinner.

There was not a woman in the neighborhood who would not have been glad to set dinner before a party of searchers. Not a woman who had not been frightening her little ones more carefully about wandering into the tall grass, such helpless slight persons, with that tall menace always waiting at hand for them. Marget McDowell had all the morning been looking from time to time down the road, hoping to see a horseman coming with good news. But no news came. She served the men. They ate in silence, hungrily. Having finished, they went out and lay down in the shade of the house. Most of them slept. Davie McDowell sat next to Wully, smoking vile home-grown tobacco in a stern old pipe. Beyond him Geordie Sproul went on theorizing in a lullabying voice. Wully was half asleep himself when he heard him saying;

"If we knew the girl to ask, we might learn something." "Girl" when he pronounced it, rhymed with peril. He was a canny man, Geordie, and Wully was instantly awake.

"Hoots!" replied Davie. "He was never one to run after girils!"

"Was he not!" answered Geordie. His voice was so suggestive, so leering, that Wully sat up.

"It's one o'clock!" he hastened to announce. "We ought to be going on!" He woke all the lads up. They started by twos and threes back towards the creek.

Wully might easily have asked Geordie privately what he meant by that comment of his. But he didn't dare. Was it possible that Geordie, that unconsidered man, knew anything about Chirstie? Or about Wully McLaughlin's private affairs? He must have meant something, and Wully wanted intensely to know what it was. Doubtless Davie McDowell would presently be inquiring, for gossip's sake. But Wully assured himself that if Geordie really knew anything about the truth of the matter, he would never dare to tell it. Nor would he have dared to hint before Wully that he knew it! Only—would he not dare? Men dared strange things, nowadays, it seemed! Even cowards like Peter Keith! They seemed to think Wully McLaughlin a soft, easy-going man. They would speedily find out their mistake! They would get rid of the idea that he was a man with whom one might safely take unspeakable liberties. If only he might have the fortune, the one chance in a thousand, or ten thousand, to come upon that damned snake, lying somewhere hidden.... Exhausted, sore in muscles and mind, he went on through the breathless thicket.

At four he came again to the water's edge, and saw Chirstie's brother Dod just coming out from a swim. He threw himself down under a great linden tree for a rest, and under his hand he saw Dod's hat full of choice blackberries. Dod was undoubtedly preparing to make himself as comfortable as possible. He was weary enough to defy the world, and relinquish his pretenses of being a man. He made his decision known flatly.

"I'm not going back into that!" he announced. "I'm through!" It was plain that his swim hadn't cooled his temper much.

Wully repressed a smile. Dod was extremely thin. The ridges of his ribs showed under his skin, which gleamed white and wet in places, in vivid contrast to his tanned arms and neck, and he was stepping along gingerly to avoid thorns, lifting his bony legs high. One of his eyelids had been scratched so that his eye was swollen shut.

"You've done enough," said Wully. "You've got a bad eye there!"

The boy struggled wet into his shirt and overalls and stretching out near Wully, began dividing the berries. Wully had to notice, how men's zeal to help Libby Keith vanished as she grew distant. In her presence, in the presence of Motherhood itself, so to speak, they were shame-faced and eager, deploring their helplessness, as men are while their wives labor in childbirth. But away from her agony, they forgot ... as men do after labor is over ... and turned again to their own comfort. Dod broke the silence surprisingly.

"Chirstie'd be glad if he was dead!" he said, resentfully.

"Why, Dod!" exclaimed Wully.

"She would that! She hates him!"

"He's your cousin, lad!"

"He's as much your cousin as he is mine! She can't endure the sight of him!"

Wully sat up. He looked at Dod. He had thought of him always as a child. He was a big, tall boy now. Fourteen years old he was, and doubtless able to put two and two together. How much did he know? He must have heard people talking. Wully suddenly wondered why he had not always been afraid of Dod. To be sure, he had always been careful to keep on the good side of his little brother-in-law.

"He never done us any good!" Dod spoke vindictively.

Now what could he mean by that? Wully was getting excited. Why had the boy so great a resentment against Peter, instead of against him, Wully, under the circumstances? Dod's sudden and apparent preference for Wully at once grew odious to him. Dod had chosen that morning to work with Wully. He was always choosing to work with him. Why? It seemed unaccountable to him that he had never been suspicious of the lad before. Wully dared not say to him;

"Well, he never did you any special harm, did he?" Suppose Dod would blurt out what he knew! He said, confusedly;

"Look here, Dod. You oughtn't to talk that way! Not at this time, I mean—you can't speak ill of the dead, you know."

"I ain't said half the truth!"

"You know how Aunt Libby feels!" Wully urged stupidly. "And Chirstie wouldn't like you to say that—not now, you know—"

"Old fool!" commented Dod. Undoubtedly he was meaning his aunt. Wully couldn't approve of such sentiments in one so young.

"You ought to go home and get something put on your eye!" he began, hastily. "And if you feel like working in the morning, you come back with me again!"

Dod went away, unsolved and uncomforting. Hour by hour the seekers, conquered by fatigue and the growing assurance of futility, stopped more often for breath. They had time to gather more and more berries, from bushes which obviously hid no dying man. They refreshed themselves more and more frequently in waters wherein no drowned man was floating. Most of them went home in time for their neglected chores that night, discouraged, hopeless.

Isobel McLaughlin was still at the Keiths', detained by Libby's need of her. Libby, though she used men easily for her purpose, was not a woman to depend on them. Her mild old husband could give her no sufficient support in her affliction. He had never been a mother. He was just a man whom life and marriage had left blinking, swallowing as best he might his realization of his own unimportance in the universe. Libby would have Isobel with her. So Chirstie in her mother-in-law's house put the younger McLaughlins and Bonnie Wee Johnnie to bed, and came out to sit on the doorstep with her weary and outraged husband. Presently she asked him wistfully;

"Do you really think he's dead, Wully?"

"It's getting to look like it."

She gave a great sigh. If only she could be sure he was dead!

"You don't think he's just gone away now?" she continued.

"Nobody thinks that now."

"Why don't they?"

"It don't look reasonable to them."

"It looks reasonable enough to me."

He longed to reassure her.

"If he had gone back to town, he would have had to stop in some place to get something to eat. He didn't stop anywhere."

She slapped away a mosquito.

"But if he didn't stop as he came, why should he stop going back?"

"He may have stopped at a dozen places coming, and found no one at home. He may have gone to his mother's when she was at the picnic. That's what she keeps wailing about—because she wasn't there when he came!"

In the silence of the starlight, she gave a great sigh.

"It's all my fault!" she declared.

He was too tired to listen to that.

"Our fault, indeed!" he answered sharply. "We never told him to come sneaking back and get lost, did we! We didn't tell him never to write to his mother."

"I didn't say it was your fault. I said mine! Really, all auntie's trouble seems to come from me. Sometimes I just seem to make everybody miserable." She had been wondering what she was to do if Peter's death made Wully's lie permanent.

"Havers, Chirstie!" he remonstrated, "her trouble comes through her own foolishness. She was never less than a fool about that—that—"

"She was always good to me, Wully, whatever you say. I mind how she stayed with me after mother's death. If she's been foolish about Peter, she's paid well for it."

"So've you!" said Wully. "He's dead, I tell you!" And there was another thing to be said. Wully might be bewildered, uncomfortable, frustrated, cheated of any assurance of safety for Chirstie. But there was one triumph, and not a small one. "He's dead. And we never speak ill of the dead, Chirstie!"

She understood his triumph. She would have been glad to have him dead, and not putting Wully into danger. She would be relieved, too, of that sense of terror, if she saw him dead. Then she thought of that great sinful lie, and of Isobel McLaughlin.

"I can't tell what to wish!" she sighed miserably. "It can't end well. I wish they'd find him dead. But if he's dead, how can I ever...." Her voice gave way to despair.

"Yes," repeated Wully. "How can you ever...." They sat silent.

"You never can!" he said securely, at length.

CHAPTER XVIII

The night after the second day's search Libby Keith had gone to bed for a while, because she was unable longer to stand up. Again she had risen when the moon rose, and Isobel McLaughlin, hearing her in the kitchen, had risen to find her washing out a shallow tin milk pan. Libby had managed to make her purpose known. Her voice was altogether gone now, after so much calling to her Lammie, and she was starting out with the pan and the poker, so that when her Peter heard the noise she was making, he would know that help was near. With Isobel following her as best she might, she beat back and forth up and down the roads again till morning, when she fell exhausted near the McCreaths' at dawn, so that they had to hitch up and take her home. And lying in the wagon, she muttered and moaned. Isobel understood that sometimes she was simply saying her son's name. Sometimes she was trying to tell what a good lad he had always been. And sometimes she said, "Only forty yards from home"; sometimes, "A wee'an's bones!" But some of the neighbors gathering had heard her pan's din and praying, and the hunt was on again, before the sun was well up.

Later that morning Isobel McLaughlin sat telling Wully about that night, in the Keiths' kitchen, whispering, looking carefully towards the door of the room where Libby was supposed to be resting. She was sitting by the breakfast table. On the red cloth three cold half-drunk cups of tea told how negligible a thing food was in that household. Suddenly she said passionately:

"Wully, you've got to bring him home alive to-day!" and with that, to her son's consternation, she burst into great weeping.

Wully, fearing the sight of his aunt's grief, hadn't wanted to come that morning to the accursed house. But his father had asked him to, looking at him, Wully thought, with an unusual sharpness, so that hurriedly, to avoid suspicion, he had said he would come. He had dreaded the errand. But he had never foreseen this. He never remembered seeing his mother cry before, not even at the time of his brother's death, though she must have wept then. And now—well, it was no wonder she was undone, after forty-eight hours of such nightmare. But he was beside himself at the sight. He got up and strode around the room, at his wits' end. Life was upside down. Chirstie at his mother's broken and nervous from her shock; his aunt raving mad; his mother crying noisily....

"You think he's alive, don't you, Wully?" she was asking him, between sobs and sniffles. "You don't think he's dead, do you?" He marveled to see how utterly she shared his aunt's grief. She could scarcely have wanted more Peter's return, if he had been her own son. He answered staunchly;

"No! Of course he's not dead, mother! A man don't die from sleeping outdoors a couple of nights in July!"

"You don't think—he's fallen into some slough—and drowned, do you?"

"No, mother! Of course not! He's around some place, drunk, likely! Don't cry, mother!"

"How could he be alive—some place—and let us all go on hunting him?"

Suddenly she added, with a greater sob, lifting her head;

"Wully, if Peter's alive, and just letting his mother think he's lost, we ought to whip him when he's found! Every man that's spent a day hunting him ought to give him a—beating! Wully, he'd never do that! I think he's—he's dead!"

"Mother, mother! Don't you cry so! It'll be all right. They'll find him soon!"

"If you don't find him soon, Auntie will go mad!"

Wully could have cried aloud the conviction that came flooding over him that minute: "If we do find him alive, and I get my hands on him, you will go mad!" He began, like a child begging;

"Mother, don't you stay here! You come home with me! It's enough to kill you, staying here with Auntie! Let someone else stay a while. Why can't Aunt Flora stay with her to-day? You come on home with me!"

"I can stay. She wants me. I can stand anything, if only he's found. Wully!" she cried, raising a face toward him distorted with tears, "don't you know where he is?"

If Chirstie had been there to see that face, she would have thought that now, at last, Isobel McLaughlin was betraying her secret, so visibly did forbidden questions tremble on her tongue. Wully only said, soothingly, indulgently;

"If I knew where he was, don't you think I would go there and find him? Mother, you need a rest. You haven't had enough sleep!"

His mother sat bending towards him, beseeching him with all her soul to tell her the truth. But not one of her passionate unspoken entreaties reached him. It never occurred to him that she might know. He sat looking at her sympathetically, troubled that she spoke words of such unusual foolishness, being overwrought by all that had befallen her.

"Won't you come home with me?" he said again.

"No, I won't!" she said, with some asperity, and put her head down on her arms on the table, and went on crying.

He rode away to his place in the hunt, and underneath all his greetings, his short and dry comments on the day's possibilities, there stayed with him a troubled sense of pity for his mother. She was getting old. And he had treated her badly. Sometimes he even thought that he had treated her very badly in that affair, even though it was over now. All those hours, those murderous hours of the last days, he had never given her a thought. He hadn't stopped in his hating long enough to imagine how deeply, how terribly, he was about to wound her. If he came upon Peter, and killed him—as he must—what would his mother do? How brokenly even now she grieved for Aunt Libby! What would her grief be like then? The thought sickened him. He said to himself bitterly that he was so tired, so confused, that if he came upon that damned snake alone, he'd likely shake hands with him and let him go! He scarcely knew what he was doing.

All the parties had changed places that day. It seemed impossible for men to hunt repeatedly through the same place with any heart. It was a fifteen-hour nightmare. Added to the growing sense of futility, of frustration, of physical exhaustion, and the burden of the heat, Wully had that uneasiness about his mother to harrow him. He had gone with the men who were searching through his own lands, that day, through the low land where he had so prayerfully hoped to bury his enemy. And he seldom was allowed even to hunt about alone. Someone or other was always near him, so that if he came upon that—that— he would have no chance to work his quick will upon him safely.

The fourth day they gathered again, going over routes that seemed hopeless. Peter, alive or dead, was simply in no place within miles. Not a little pebble, even, remained unturned now. The older men were sustaining themselves on strong drink more or less soberly, and the younger ones considerably less soberly. The first day of the alarm had been something of a picnic to thoughtless youngsters used to solitary hoeing, something of a diversion to men accustomed to plowing alone from dawn to darkness. But the excitement was dying away. Paths were beaten roads, and roads great wide highways. Miles of untrodden sloughs had become familiar ground, and acres of cryptic underbrush had become overworked monotony. What the slough had swallowed up, it would keep. If the tall grasses had treasures hidden, only the winter could bring low the tall grasses. The crowd dwindled.

First those from the farther and less concerned settlements went back to their work, protesting they would all be watching, that they would keep a wide and long lookout always, for any signs of news. They regretted that their harvests were urgent. They departed. Then day by day members of the clan returned to neglected fields. John McLaughlin kept his children hunting, and as for the Squire he vowed he would never stop. His sporting blood was up. For nine days more Wully and his father went again and again from impossible clue to foolish conjecture. Wully's belief grew constantly stronger that Peter had simply gone back to wherever he had come from. But how he had done it on a road where one passer-by made a day memorable, he couldn't imagine. It suggested a devilish cunning, a subtility not to be lightly reckoned with, a persistence that made an honest man's blood boil. To his praying mother he affirmed that Peter was alive. To his dreading wife, he proclaimed that certainly he was dead. The whole desire of his life was to know which statement was true.

Their wheat called them, at length. It was almost their year's income, and to its whitening invitation they must listen. They took down their cradles, and fell upon it. Then they together went and harvested poor old Uncle Keith's crop for him. He was no farmer at any time, and now too weakened by sorrow to save his wheat. Libby kept her bed for days together, and for many days Isobel McLaughlin hung over her, trying to save her sanity.

However much Chirstie shrank from it, she had to leave her mother-in-law's well-filled house and go back to the loneliness of her own. Her harvesters must have food cooked and ready for them. Sometimes one of Wully's little sisters stayed a few days with her, sometimes a little brother. Wully had told his mother simply that since the day Chirstie had fainted there alone on the Fourth of July, he wouldn't have her left without company. His mother had listened simply, searchingly, wondering unhappily about many suggestive circumstances.

And all the time Chirstie kept insisting she wasn't afraid. Not she! No indeed! But she never got Wully to believe her. He knew why she brought lunches so often to the field, and why she loitered about with him, forgetting her housework. He saw why she had suddenly become so keen about shooting, why day by day she potted away at worthless small birds, which formerly her pity would never have let her shoot. Let her say what she would, she was so much afraid that her very eyes had changed. Never before had they had that way of shifting instantly under her long lashes. Never before since she had been his wife had they had that haunted expression. She was bitterly afraid, and he was unable to reassure her. He could do nothing. It was as if some invisible unconquerable rattler crawled about in that little house where his wife and baby had been so happy. It seemed that all his safety lay in crushing down a great, uplifted club upon an intangible enemy.

The green months passed at length, and the golden ones were all but gone. John went back to Chicago, and the young children started back to school through goldenrod and wild sunflowers, down paths with fuchsia-colored wild asters, amethyst, blue, and pink. Chirstie was alone, perforce. Occasionally she had a visitor. Aunt Libby came oftener than anyone else. She was better again, able to spend day after day on horseback, going about from neighbor to neighbor, and calling, as she went, to ease her heart in the lonely places, "Lammie, Lammie!" She came often to Wully's to see Bonnie Wee Johnnie. She had taken a notion that he was like her Peter. He ran about now, and it seemed not strange to his mother that a woman should ride miles for the pleasure of watching him. She taught him carefully to tolerate Aunt Libby's extravagant caresses. Wully's sisters were entirely indignant when they heard that Aunt Libby thought the baby looked like her son. But as they afterwards remarked, it was just like Aunt Libby to say that the prettiest child in the neighborhood resembled her blessed Peter.

CHAPTER XIX

The year's calendar of color was almost at an end; only white was left for it now. The fields had been black. They had grown green, shyly, softly. They had given themselves up to bold greenness. They had achieved their golden maturity. They had reveled in gold, and dazzled by it. They had faded into dullness and browns. They died and lay withered. Snows would come soon for their burial. The morning's white frosts were the promise of it.

Chirstie must keep the doors shut now, for the baby's sake. With doors shut the house seemed a trap, a trap from whose windows she had often to be looking to reassure herself. Out of doors she felt safer, freer. So she said that the baby must have more air, and she took him day after day to the field where Wully was husking corn. Since the mosquitoes were no longer hungry, the baby's face was free for the first time in months from red blotches. He grew rosier and rosier in the cornfield. He looked so blooming that Chirstie said she just had to take him visiting, to show him to the neighbors. That was another excuse for not staying at home alone, another which Wully pretended to be deceived by.

It happened that one morning Squire McLaughlin, riding past, saw a flock of wild turkeys alight in her dooryard, and leaving his horse, he crept toward the house, to borrow Wully's gun, and bring down a bird for dinner. He had all but gained the house, when out of the door shot Chirstie, crying out a cry unintelligible. Out of the door and down towards the corn she flew. It gave him a startle, as he said afterwards. He didn't know what terrible thing might have happened. He started after her. He called to her questioningly. She never lessened her pace. He said later that he had never seen a woman run as fast as she did. He could scarcely keep within sight of her among the dead cornstalks. He happened to see Wully hear her cry of anguish, and his swift, leaping answer. The Squire called to him, and Wully heard him, and stopped, confusedly, and began calling to his wife.

"It's Uncle Wully, Chirstie! It's only Uncle Wully!" he called to her, as if he had some great news to give her. She stumbled against him, panting and white, and the Squire hurried on to them, in consternation. There the three of them stood, breathless, excited, looking blankly from one to the other.

"Whatever's the trouble?" the Squire gasped, recovering first.

Chirstie had grown red with relief and humiliation.

"Oh!" she stammered, confusedly. "Oh! I just thought—I thought you were—a tramp!"

"You were never running from me, Chirstie!" he exclaimed.

"Yes, I was! I just thought—you came up so quietly—I didn't know—" She paused, and looked at her husband beseechingly. "I got a fright," she murmured.

Wully knew what she thought. Pitiful, she was. Just pitiful. Standing there trembling, ashamed, trying to cover her folly. Let the Squire laugh as loud as he would. Let him fill the prairies with his relief and amusement. He said he had never seen anything so amazing. Him to be chasing her, frightening her more and more! He didn't know he looked so much like a tramp! The birds must have been as frightened as she had been. She had spoiled a fine shot for him. He had supposed the house was on fire, at least.

"I hope they were scared! I don't want them shot! I'm taming them. They come every morning," she retorted. She wanted to make him forget what she had done. He stood laughing at her indulgently, amused because she was a pretty thing. "Come back to the house and I'll give you a slice of cold turkey that father shot yesterday. Wasn't it a good bird, Wully!"

She started back towards the house. Wully went with them. After all, it was nearly noon. She begged the Squire not to tell what had happened. She had been having fever, and it would only worry Isobel McLaughlin to know she was so flighty. He promised, but she saw from his face he was already making a fine yarn about how he terrified women. She knew he wouldn't be able to keep it to himself.

That hour Wully came to a great decision. He had been considering for some time a proposition a cousin of his had made to him, a son of the Squire's. Next spring the railroad would have completed its track to its next western terminal, and the new station which would become a town, was to be but three miles from Wully's farm. From that town, all the supplies that settlers must have would be hauled a hundred miles west. What they would need first and always would be lumber. The Squire's John wanted Wully to leave his farm, and start with him selling lumber. Wully would have a little money, and the cousin had some, and for a great wonder, they knew where they could borrow more.

The money they could borrow was a thing which even in those days startled men's minds. Wully's cousin John had an aunt who had come with her husband, a miller, from Scotland, and had settled some hundred miles away, where Houghton could get work in a mill. His employer was an old Yankee of some wealth. In the winter of sixty, the old man had decided suddenly and irrevocably, to sell the mill, and the Houghtons had wondered where they would be able to find work anew. The miller had ordered Houghton to find a purchaser. His orders were always imperious and startling. Houghton had set about the task, and had persuaded two men to buy the plant, which he promised to manage. They had come and looked the place over carefully. But just as the papers were to be signed, they had changed their minds, so that when the miller was already rejoicing erratically because of his freedom from responsibility he found himself still encumbered with a business.

He was beside himself with anger. He was determined to sell that mill at once, without delay. He wouldn't wait. So it came about that almost before he knew what he was doing, Houghton himself had bought that mill, with fifty thousand bushels of wheat for fifty cents a bushel, paying down for it all the money he could raise, which was eighty-five dollars. The miller had simply bullied him into the bargain. Houghton was overwhelmed with the burden of so great a debt. He felt that he had been basely taken advantage of. Then in a few weeks came the war. The first thing he knew he sold his wheat for three times what he paid for it. Wealth has perhaps seldom fallen so suddenly upon a man so little dreaming of it. Houghton bought at once ten thousand acres of Iowa land, and nowadays, his sons who go round and round this stuffy little stupid globe in their yachts, berate his memory yawningly because he didn't buy a hundred thousand acres. He was the man who would lend two soldiers of his kin a few hundred dollars to begin business.

Wully had thought before the bomb of Peter's return that farming was no life for Chirstie. She was no tireless woman like his mother. Malaria was a hard thing for young wives and nursing mothers. Wully had often wished that in some way he might make her necessary work lighter. And now that this intolerable menace of violence hung over their home, it seemed best altogether to leave it. He knew what his father would say to the idea that a man getting a dollar and seventy cents for wheat, should leave his land. His father thought a man who left off tilling his land to dig gold out of it a poor shiftless creature. None of those who would advise him so vigorously against his contemplated course could foresee that wheat, that brought so great a price that fall, would the next year be selling for thirty cents. But after Chirstie's flight from her uncle, Wully didn't care what they advised. He wouldn't have his wife trembling. He would give his answer to his cousin at once. They would move to town.

A Sabbath some weeks later Wully and Chirstie and Bonnie Wee Johnnie were at Isobel McLaughlin's for dinner, and the Squire was there, with several of his smaller children, and the McNairs. The women and the girls were clearing away the dinner things in the big kitchen, and the men had withdrawn to the Sabbath parlor, where the best rag carpet was, and the basket quilt spread on the bed. In the stiff propriety of that room they had been talking with less cordiality than usual. McNair had only scorn for Wully's folly in leaving his farm, and Wully had no great patience with his father-in-law's disapproval. He had been saying that he would get a renter, and McNair had commented scoffingly that that was a likely thing. Who would rent land that could be had almost for the asking? The place would go back to weeds, he averred. Wully protested that he never would allow that. Somebody would come along glad to get a bit of broken ground for a crop. If not, he would drive back and forth from town every day, and care for it himself. That would be great farming, McNair had remarked, significantly. Farming was just now beginning to amount to something. Look at the years they had spent miles from markets. Consider the money they had lost before the war when they had got for their produce greenbacks which depreciated in value before they could get them spent. And now when the iron horse was here to serve them, when their millennium was at hand, Wully was going to quit farming! (They never called the railroad anything but the iron horse at that time and place.) Hadn't they prayed for its coming? Hadn't they waited and paid in their hard-earned dollars for its advent? John McLaughlin himself had contributed three hundred dollars when the subscription paper went round for funds to help out the prospective builders of the road, and McNair himself had been moved to give a hundred and fifty. Well, that money had been wasted. That company had failed. But now—Ah, now, the day was at hand. They had the land. The nation needed food. The railroad solved their last problem. How rich they were to be! They sat exulting in hope of years that were to be born starved and dying. And now the young men talked of selling lumber!

The Keiths came driving in, and the men joined the women in the kitchen to welcome them. Even the children playing at the door followed them in. Libby Keith took off her hat and wrap and gave them to a niece. She was more gray, more flabby than ever now, and her eyes were dull and brooding. But just as she went to sit down, Bonnie Wee Johnnie came in, and she saw him, and instantly her face grew soft and warm with tenderness, and her eyes grew bright. She ran and knelt down on the floor, and folded her arms about him.

"Oh, the bonnie wee laddie!" she murmured, kissing him. "Oh, the gay lit'lin'!" And then, kneeling as she was, she turned her face up towards her old husband and exclaimed,

"Look, John! Is he not like him?"

The unimportant John, peering intently out of his kindly old face, smiled down on them, sighing.

"As like as two peas!" he said gently.

Then Libby, fumbling with one hand while her other held the little boy, pulled from a pocket in her voluminous cotton skirt a picture in a little case. No other woman of her class had dreamed in Scotland of aping the gentry to such an extent as having a picture of her children made. But Libby Keith had, of course, gone without food to save the necessary money. She could starve more easily than lose the remembrance of those tender child faces of hers. She opened the case, and looked at it intently for only a moment. Then she handed it to Isobel McLaughlin.

"Look at this, Isobel! You said he was more like Wully!"

Isobel took the picture, and looked at it. Tears came unexpectedly into her eyes. There before her was Libby's Davie, a little, innocent, broad-faced laddie, with his arm protestingly around his sister Flora, who, with her head shyly on one side, looked out at the world with wondering round eyes. And seated before them, on a stool with fringe, one leg crossed under him, sat little Peter, with a plaid cap lying proudly in his lap. Isobel blinked away her tears. "Ah, Davie was like that!" she murmured. And then she turned and looked at her grandson still in Libby's arms. He had on his best Sunday dress that his stepgrandmother had made for him, of scarlet wool nunsveiling, a little frock that Chirstie keeps to this day folded immaculately away. It was low in the neck, and had no sleeves to hide the soft dimpled arms. Around the neck and the flaring skirt were three rows of very narrow black velvet ribbon. Chirstie had curled his hair that morning around her finger. The curls at the back of his head were still in shape, and the long one that came down the top of his head to his forehead, disarranged as it was, still showed what a soft, sweet thing it must have been before his romp with the children. And there in the frame Isobel looked at what might have been the picture of the child before her, the very forehead, the same childish nose. Only little Johnnie had a winsome way of screwing his mouth into smiles which he must have got from his secret grandfather Keith who, quite unadmired, stood watching him indulgently.

Isobel McLaughlin said gently;

"You're right, Libby. He's like it. Peter is a McLaughlin if ever there was one." And having taken away any cause for apprehension that Chirstie might have had, and having given her husband's family a little knock from which under the circumstances, the two McLaughlin men were not able to defend themselves, she handed the picture calmly to Chirstie, saying again;

"It might have been our baby's picture." She never again had any doubt about the paternity of the child. And so simply had she justified the resemblance, that Chirstie studied the picture unabashed, with a natural interest. The picture was handed from one to another, and Wully, when he got it, studied it intently.

No one noticed him doing it. Libby Keith had sighed again, and said, just about that time;

"'To them that hath, it shall be given.' Them that has sons, has grandsons."

Wully looked up from the picture to her, and wondered if it would have comforted her to know that the child so brutally begotten was indeed her grandson. Not that it made any difference, of course. He wouldn't tell her in any case. He hated that little picture. It had possibilities against which he couldn't fight. And the women were saying to the baby;

"Say 'Aunt Libby,' Johnnie. Come on, now! Say 'Aunt Libby.' Say it, baby! Look, he's going to say it!"

They had reason to think so. Johnnie prepared for action. He pursed up his red lips. He looked around upon his admirers, complacently, happily. All eyes were upon him. He let them wait a moment. Then he manipulated his lips more earnestly. The great moment was at hand.

"Pr-r-r-r-r!" he articulated proudly. "Pr-r-r!"

Various aunties dived for him, rewarding him with laughter and huggings, enthusiastically. Was there ever so silly a baby, ever a bairn so lovable, they asked. It occurred to Wully casually that perhaps the secure son of Wully McLaughlin was a more fortunate being than the unfathered offspring of Peter Keith would have been.

CHAPTER XX

The corn was husked. The year's work in the fields was over. Wully had sold from sixty of the acres for which his father had paid two hundred and ten dollars in sixty-four, wheat worth three thousand and sixty dollars. He had his house all paid for now. He owned three hundred acres of land, some of it a bit farther west, where a bushel of wheat still bought an acre of the faithful soil. His little pines had grown steadily, and his orchard, now that the grasses and weeds were frosted, was visible to the naked eye from the house, a lot of little switches ready to stand bravely against the gales. Everything prospered with him. Everything, except for that shadow of evil that clouded their lives hatefully. Every day Wully's mind dwelt futilely upon the problem of Peter Keith's fate. And Chirstie's eyes, he observed, still shifted apprehensively under their tender lids.

And what was he to do now, when he must go to the timber for his winter's supply of wood? When he must leave early in the morning, and return at nightfall? He couldn't leave her alone. He had remarked to one neighbor and another that he wanted some man to bring his wood home for hire. But he found no man willing to do his work. Chirstie would have to take the baby and go to her father's or his mother's. She didn't want to do that. Either Wully would have to take her back and forth daily—and that was a difficult thing under the circumstances—or else she would have to stay away for days together, and then Wully would come home to a cold house and no food ready. They dreaded those days.

He finished the corn on a Wednesday, and on Thursday they were to have a great lark. They were to go to town together for the first time. He had a wagonload of prairie chickens to sell, which ought to bring at least ten dollars—silly birds he had caught almost without effort as he husked his corn. Everything was ready. For one day they would put aside all their misgivings, and be happy together. They were enjoying what seemed to be a second Indian summer, bland days for riding across the country. And there was that spring-seat ready for Chirstie's comfort. Moreover, she was to have a new coat. Wully had wanted to get her one the fall before, but she had said that there were so many things that they had to buy for their house that they really couldn't afford the coat. She still protested that she really didn't need it. But Wully was the more determined because he suspected she wore her mother's old wrap for the principle of the thing. As if she needed to act humble! He wouldn't have it!

The store in which they found the right coat finally was narrow and dark and full of dull necessities, mittens and milk-crocks, grim boots, and grimmer tobacco. Wully hated the clerk the moment he saw him fix upon Chirstie eyes that narrowed expressively. Nevertheless, the odious man brought out from some dark recess behind the main room the very garment they were searching for.

"Put this on," he urged familiarly. She put it on. It was a green thing, so dark a green it was almost black, and rich-looking, short in front, and falling, mantle-wise, well down over her skirts behind. It had rich fringe on it, and intricate frogs for fastenings. Wully would have forestalled the clerk, and buttoned it for her, but his fingers were awkward and helpless in such a task. So the man did it, standing as near her as he dared. But when she stood forth arrayed, Wully's annoyance was forgotten. He heaved a sigh of satisfaction.

He saw again with surprise how garments change women. She was scarcely the same being who had walked in, in that faded old dingy wrap. This coat was made for her, beyond a doubt She asked the price.

"Sixteen dollars."

She sighed and began undoing it. She would look at some others, she said. The man left them.

"Don't you like it?" demanded Wully.

"It's too fine for me. Sixteen dollars!" she commented.

"It's not too fine. It's becoming, Chirstie!"

"But sixteen dollars!" she exclaimed, as if that settled the matter.

"Ah, sixteen dollars isn't going to break us up!" Wully urged, determinedly. "It's a grand coat. It's nobby." He was at a loss to express his admiration for the garment. He only felt vaguely that it looked like Glasgow.

"But sixteen dollars, Wully! The idea!"

"You'll have it, anyway."

"I will not!" She was indignant "Why, Wully, your coat, your overcoat was only ten last winter!"

"But I hadn't any red dress to match. Nor any feather!"

The man had come back.

"If you want something cheap now, for your wife—"

"I don't want anything cheap!" said Wully, "We'll take this."

Chirstie stood examining it inside and out. She was wondering what her father would say to such a coat.

She wore the nobby coat away. Wully carried the old garment. He had been gay, almost hilarious all the morning, ever since selling the prairie chickens so well. And now as he looked at his stunning wife, walking demurely along in such grandeur, his spirits rose higher. He watched people look at her. He chuckled to see them.

They walked down the busy little street. He left the old coat at the hotel. She saw a shawl she admired, and he wanted to buy it for her. But she was thinking how nice it would be for his mother, a little soft fine shawl like that. He wondered that he hadn't thought of that himself. They bought the shawl, and went on down the street. They came to a place where tintypes were taken. It came over him like a flash.

"We'll go in and have our pictures taken!" he exclaimed.

"Oh," she said hesitating. "How much will it cost?"

"Oh, nothing much!" he exclaimed. He made her go in with him. There was a picture, was there, he was thinking, that made Wee Johnnie look like the son of that snake? Well, there should soon be another that made him look like another man's son. Chirstie had never had her likeness taken. But Wully had had his made in St. Louis, to be sent to his mother. He knew how to walk in and have the thing done grandly.

He sat down in a chair, and put the baby on one knee, paternally. On the other knee he spread out a great hand. Chirstie took her place behind him, her hand on his shoulder, her feather curling down over her hat, her new sixteen-dollar coat, her wine-colored skirts showing bravely. And when that was done, he made her sit down with the baby on her knee, for a picture of just the mother and son. And then a further happy thought came to him. He sat down and took the baby, and cuddled his face right up against his own, and demanded a picture.

"It ain't usual," the photographer protested. "I can't take a picture like that! It ain't usual!"

"This ain't no usual baby!" Wully replied chuckling. Who could have made a statement more paternal than that? "I want his face against mine!" And he got the picture taken that way, in the end.

They sought the street again. Chirstie was rather overcome by her husband's grandness. He had such a worldly air—commanding people about. He kept getting more imperious, more happy all the time though he was entirely sober. After a while, when it was growing dusk, he spied a friend on the street, just going into his office.

"That's Mr. Knight, Chirstie! You remember! The man that drove me home that time! I'll take you to see him!" He wanted to show her to everybody.

They went into an office having not only a kerosene lamp, but a lamp with a rich green shade, most luxurious, most metropolitan-looking. Chirstie was shy, and Mr. Knight puzzled for a moment.

"I'm McLaughlin," Wully explained. "The soldier you drove out to Harmony, two years ago. I was sick, you remember!"

Mr. Knight's face lighted up with recognition.

"Come in, McLaughlin!" he said heartily. "I didn't recognize you! Sit down!" Around a table at one end of the room, men were playing cards, well dressed men, who paused and looked up, and continued looking at the newcomers. A tall wide bookcase screened off one corner into something like a private office and to this Mr. Knight led them.

"My wife!" Wully said proudly, as he seated them.

"Your wife? Your baby? Why, it doesn't seem possible! How the time gets away! And where did you find her?" he asked, so frankly pleased with her appearance that she blushed more deeply than she had at his first remark.

"She's from out there! From Harmony."

"She is," he exclaimed. He continued looking at her. "Well, I always said that that was a remarkable country. A remarkable country," he drawled.

Wully was delighted. Knight was a man whose opinion was valuable, a prosperous man, a man dressed as men dress in cities, whose interest he felt was not merely assumed for political ends. "How's your mother?" he went on. He asked about the children, and the crops, and the new town which was to be near them. Finally he said:

"Well you certainly don't look much like you did that morning. You were sick. Skin and bones. Do you remember?"

"Do I remember!" exclaimed Wully. "Will I ever forget!" He turned to his wife. "Chirstie, I was sitting right down there by the elevator, where the sidewalk is built up high, you know. I wasn't sitting, either, I was lying stretched out, to try to keep from throwing up! I thought I'd seen Jimmy Sproul out there, and I'd ride home with him, and when I hurried up to him, it wasn't Jimmy at all! It just made me sick! And I was lying there when Mr. Knight came along, and began asking me what was the matter of me. He said he would take me home. 'How far is it?' you asked, and when I said twenty-six miles, you said, 'Oh! Twenty-six miles!' Naturally. That made some difference. My heart sank, as they say. Or maybe it was my breakfast trying to get out. Anyway, I had a pang of some kind. And you said, 'You wait here!' And pretty soon along you came with those grays! I tell you I felt better even then. I got better all the way home. Every step. It seemed that morning as if I couldn't wait another minute to start home!"

"Naturally!" remarked Mr. Knight, looking again with a smile, at Chirstie.

"Oh, I didn't know her then! If I had known her I'd have started home crawling! Have you got those grays yet?" asked Wully, suddenly curious.

"No, I haven't." The man smiled reminiscently. "I wish I had, sometimes. A Chicago man came along and wanted them. He was determined to have them. I let them go for a half section of land in Lyons County. I wouldn't have done it," he added confidently, "only my son had a baby born a day or two before that. I thought the land would be a good thing to keep for the child. How old is this little fellow?" He snapped his fingers invitingly towards the child.

"Oh, he's—a year or two. Something like that, isn't he?" he asked his wife.

"Tut, tut, McLaughlin! You need experience! When they're young like that the women count them in months. Don't they, Mrs. McLaughlin?" he appealed.

"How old is your grandchild?" Wully parried boldly.

"Oh, mine's several months. Mine's—well, he's got two teeth already!" And they laughed. Wully hastened to safer ground. If he wasn't careful, someone might ask him when he was married.

"I'll tell you another thing I remember!" he began. "I got in on that night train, that time, you know, and I went to the hotel where we had always stayed. Sick, I was, you know! I told the man—he'd seen me a dozen times before—that I hadn't the price of a room. He'd had too much. He never even looked to see who I was. Just saw my uniform and began swearing! Wasn't going to be eaten out of house and home by a lot of begging soldiers, he said. It nearly knocked me over. I went out to the street. And I couldn't get up face enough to go some place else and ask for a bed, at first. I just sat around. Then finally I went into the Great West—that's where we all stay now when we come in. And Pierson there almost began swearing at me because I said I'd pay him later. He didn't take soldiers' last cents away from them, he said. He saw how I felt, and he went and got some milk toast made for me. And soft boiled eggs. And then, do you know what he did? He went to a room with me, and when he saw the pillows on the bed, he went and got me a pair of good pillows from some place. I hadn't slept on a pillow for I don't know how long! A man notices those things when he's most dead, I tell you! Milk toast, and pillows, by Jiminy! And in the morning he sat and fed me such a lot of breakfast—no wonder I had trouble! I felt as if I'd never get enough to eat."

Mr. Knight made him go on talking. They sat there till the street was dark. And then Wully led his wife away, right up to the hotel. And then into the dining room. It seemed lordly to her that dining room—an amazing day—and Wully most lordly and amazing of all. It was like a fine wedding trip, almost, that day.

CHAPTER XXI

They had breakfasted together before daylight, and he had gone to load the lumber he was taking home for his father, so that they might have a very early start. In the noisy, untidy hotel office she sat watching in surprise the confusion and the stir. There were crowds of women waiting near her, women like herself waiting for wagons to take them on towards the west, women with bundles and babies, and quarreling, crying young children. Chirstie's face showed how exciting the scene was to her. She looked from group to group. She considered a foreign woman with a handkerchief tied on her head, whose tiny baby coughed and wheezed distressingly. She longed to say something sympathetic to the stolid mother. But she was too shy. Between caring for her own vigorous son, and watching other women's children, the hour hurried by. Presently she saw her husband drive up, and get out to tie his horses. But before he had started for the hotel door, a stranger accosted him, and with the stranger Wully turned and went down the street. So she waited on. Two sets of youngsters quarreling drew their mothers into the fray, and Chirstie shrank away from their roughness, thoroughly shocked.

Then, before she had expected him, Wully was standing over her, reaching down for the baby. She scarcely knew him. His face was white. His eyes were shining strangely.

"What ails you?" she cried. "You're sick, Wully! What's the matter?"

"I'm all right!" he said sharply. His voice quivered with feeling. He couldn't trust himself to speak. His mouth was set in a hard line.

She rose and followed him, frightened. She got into the wagon, and he handed her the baby. He climbed up beside her, and they were off. She saw he couldn't tell her what had happened just there. She could wait—a little.

They were almost out of town now.

"Wully, what's the matter? Are you sick?"

"I'm all right!"

She was more anxious than ever. She waited till the baby was asleep in her arms, and then she laid him carefully down in the little box in which Isobel McLaughlin had taken her babies back and forth to town. Then she turned towards her husband with determination. And hesitated. He looked too stern—too fierce. She sat undecided, wretched, glancing quickly at him and then away. After a few perplexed moments, her face darkened with terror.

"Oh, I know! You're—you've seen him! You were like that on the Fourth!"

He turned toward her, trying to speak.

"Yes!" he broke forth. "I saw him dying."

"Oh, dying!" She tried to realize it. "Oh, if he's dying, then we'll be happy again!"

He said nothing. His lips worked.

"I won't have to be afraid now!" She spoke like one overcome by a great fortune. He had never imagined she had been as unhappy as that cry of hers indicated by its relief.

"Dying!" she repeated, tasting the sweetness of the word. Then, suddenly:

"How do you know? Where did you see him?"

She saw his face harden with hatred.

"Wully, are you sure he's dying? He isn't dead yet?"

"He's dying all right!"

After a moment she exclaimed:

"But how did you find him?"

"Somebody told me just as I was ready to start home."

"Oh, that man! I saw that man speaking to you. How did he know to tell you?"

"They were looking for someone to take him out home."

"Oh, they were!" That seemed to have changed the situation for her.

"You mean they asked you to bring him out?"

He didn't relish her questions.

"Yes."

"And you wouldn't do it, would you!" She approved. She clasped his arm with both hands. She rejoiced in her assurance.

His anger flamed again.

"Likely I'd bring him out with you!"

"Oh, we'll be happy now, Wully!"

But after a minute she stirred uncomfortably. He felt her face grow grave.

"Where was it you saw him, Wully?"

"In a livery stable."

"In a livery stable!" she repeated. "Dying in such a place!" Dying seemed not so sweet a word now.

"But why didn't he send word home before? Think of Aunt Libby, Wully!"

"He came in on the train last night."

"Oh!" she exclaimed, enlightened. "He wanted to get home alive!"

"What's the matter of him?" she asked again.

"Hemorrhage," said Wully, as shortly as it was possible to speak. He wouldn't tell her how he had seen that snake lying bloody, dirty, sunken helpless on a bed of straw. He urged his horses on.

She looked at him. He turned away from her troubled eyes.

After a while;

"Look here, Wully!" she faltered.

He gave her no encouragement.

"After all, he was Aunt Libby's baby!" she sighed.

"After all!" he sneered. He meant to silence her. She spoke again.

"Aunt Libby was always kind to me, Wully!"

He wouldn't answer her. He knew what was coming.

She said timidly;

"I doubt we ought to go back and get him. If he's dying, Wully! And Auntie waiting there for him!"

He said never a word.

"He may be dead before she sees him, if we don't."

"We won't!" he almost shouted. That should have settled matters.

"But what'll you tell her? She'll ask. She'll find out you wouldn't. You won't can say you saw him dying, and didn't bring him home!"

That was true. He had begun to think of that. Libby Keith would leave no detail of that death undiscovered.

"Will you say you went away and left him there to die?"

What else could he say? He certainly wouldn't tell that for one long rejoicing moment he had stood looking into the eyes that so terribly besought him—those eyes that were dying prayers, ultimate beseechings—and had turned victoriously away. He wouldn't say that he had told the men who were seeking a ride home for that snake, that he had too heavy a load for so essential a favor. He wouldn't tell how shortly he had answered them, and how hatefully turned on his heel and departed.

"Wully!" she said, after a little, with conviction, "we ought to go back and get him! We can't treat Auntie this way!"

"Can't we!" he exclaimed bitterly. "Giddup!" he cried to his horses.

He felt her wretchedness. He hardened his heart against her sentimentality. Presently she said imploringly;

"We can't do this, Wully. We must go back!"

"I will not!" He spoke passionately.

When she spoke again, it was to warn him.

"If you don't go back, I will!"

"No you won't!" he cried.

She was silent for several minutes then. He felt her bending down to see if the baby was covered. Then she sat still. She was hesitating. Then after a minute, before he could realize what was going on, she had climbed over the side of the wagon, her foot was on the hub, then, skirts and cloak and all, she had alighted, backwards, stumblingly, from the wagon. By the time he had pulled up the horses, she was the length of the wagon from him. Ignoring him, defying him, she was calling to him over her shoulder;

"He made me do evil once. You made me do evil once. But nobody can make me do it again!" Down the road she ran. "I'm going back to him!" she cried.

He had never been really angry with her before. Sometimes at first, before the baby had been born, he had grown very weary of her importunity, her determination to make him tell his mother the truth. But of late she had not done that. She had been so satisfactory—so lovely. Now his rage burst forth against her.

"Go back to him, then, if you like him so well!" He hurled the words after her, and drove on.

Even before he heard her cry of protest, he regretted his bitter taunt. Furious with himself, with her, he hurried west. Already he had begun to see the mistake of his sweet refusal. It would inevitably become known that he had seen Peter's straits, and had refused him so slight a kindness. The whole neighborhood would be asking the reason. He vowed to himself that he would not take that carcass into the wagon with his wife if all the world had to know the reason of his hatred. Such things were expected of no man. He was only human. He couldn't do a thing like that! And his wife had defied him! She had left him! Ah, and he had taunted her so unjustly, so brutally! But he had never imagined himself saying so cruel a thing to her. He had never imagined her defying him in such a fashion. That was what she thought of him, then. He made her do wrong once! Classing him with that damned—That was all the gratitude she felt for his saving of her! But then, of course, it was an awful thing he had just done. He thought of himself lying sick on the sidewalk, waiting for a chance to get home. He hardened his heart. But he had been a decent man. No violator of women! He would never do it.

He turned and looked after his deserting wife. He could see her hurrying away from him. He had an idea of shouting to her to come back—of commanding her to come back. But he knew she wouldn't heed him. He ought never to have said so hateful a thing to her. As if she could want to go back to that—He remembered how she had sat sobbing on the doorstep when he first went to her. He was glad to think of Peter Keith dying there, lonely, shrunken, filthy. He looked again after his wife. She went steadily eastward, running towards the town. But he had the baby. She would be coming back after a while!

He drove on, raging against her, trying to justify himself. He went so far that he could scarcely see her now. He might have gone on home, if there had not appeared on the horizon a team, coming towards him. Its approach was intolerable. Somebody who might know them was coming nearer. Somebody would see Wully McLaughlin riding westward, and presently overtake his wife running east! He turned around abruptly.

Facing east, he could just see her. He would quickly overtake her, and order her to get in and come home with him at once. He would never let her go to that livery stable full of drunks alone. He was getting near her.

Then a strange thing happened. He saw her stop and suddenly turn around, and come half running towards him as fast as she had run away. He kept his face hard, unrelenting. He saw when she came near that she was crying softly. She climbed quickly up when he stopped.

"I doubt he's not dying," she wept. "I can't do it! He's too strong, Wully! He's tricky!"

She cuddled against him.

"Don't cry!" he had to say.

"I won't look at him!" she sobbed. "You know I don't want to go back to him! You oughtn't to have said that! You know I don't like him! If you want to know how much I hate him, I'll tell you! It was me that shot him that time. It wasn't his foot I was aiming at, either!" She wept unrestrainedly.

"You shot him!" Wully gasped.

"He would come back! What could I do! There was no place to hide. I shot at him!"

She had shot him! She had been as desperate as that. He was horrified anew. She bent down to feel the baby's hands, to cover him more securely. She wanted to say something else, but she couldn't speak plainly because of her sobs. Yet she managed to urge the horses eastward.

"I'll never look at him!" she cried passionately. "You needn't think I like him! You oughtn't to have said that!"

"I know it, Chirstie! I oughtn't to have said such a thing. But you oughtn't to have jumped out and run away that way."

"Yes, I ought!" she retorted, swallowing, choking. "I couldn't help it. It wasn't my place to do it. But my husband wouldn't do his part! Wully, if you hurry now, hurry enough, they'll just think you've been unloading. You won't need to explain! I won't have you doing such a mean thing. I've got enough bad things to tell without that! Hurry!"

CHAPTER XXII

They had passed the bridge on their burdened way home. They had come to the place at which Chirstie had so astonishingly defied him. They had ridden together in a silence broken only by the refreshed wee Johnnie's cooing, as he bounced back and forth in his mother's lap. Wully looked covertly at his wife from time to time, in awe. She wasn't thinking now what a nice baby Peter Keith had been. Never once had she turned her face towards what was in the wagon-box, to see if it was indeed dying. Returning to town, she had instructed him, woman-like, to be sure that Peter had no weapons concealed, no way of hurting a benefactor. And Wully had unloaded his lumber raging. Caught, he was, trapped. Having to do this unspeakable thing to satisfy the sentimentality of a woman, and to save his secret from desecration. Grimly he had made sure from the doctor that there was no chance of Peter living to reveal what Wully had so well kept hidden. Coldly he had ordered the men at the stable to wash the blood from that face, from that matted beard, as if Peter was their cousin, and not his. Grudgingly he had helped them deposit the bony thing in the wagon. Covered to his head, still as a bag of meal, Peter lay there when Wully McLaughlin drove to the hotel to get his wife. And she had never once turned her head towards him.

And now, when Wully looked at her from the corner of his eyes, his own anger, his bitter hatred seemed a small thing before hers. Her face was as white as marble, and as hard, one might have thought. Her mouth was screwed tight in loathing. She sat perfectly still, looking straight ahead, tragically. She wasn't thinking of Aunt Libby now. Wully was almost afraid of her ... afraid certainly to offer her comfort.

They rode west. The sun was high now, and shone dazzlingly over the brown stretches. The horses felt the stimulus of the frosty morning. Wee Johnnie jumped about, chuckling out his absurd little meaningless words. Three miles they went; four miles. From time to time Wully turned to assure himself that his enemy lay still. He would let him die there, without lifting a finger to lengthen his life by a second. The sight of that shape under the old brown blanket inflamed his hatred. He looked, and turned quickly away, remembering always that second time Peter had dared to lay violent hands on his wife. It was that second time he could never forgive, that second time.

The baby grew restless. He complained fretfully of his mother's lack of attention. Wully gave him, almost mechanically, the ends of the lines to play with. They pleased him, for a while. Then he turned again to his mother, unable to fathom her sternness. Never before had her hands touched him so coldly. Looking right ahead of her, she would pull that little shawl tightly around him again, after he had succeeded in working his bare arms out of it, tucking him in without a kiss or any coaxing. His eyes studied her face, and found there no thought for him. He stood up in her lap. He put his arms around her neck, and stroked the forbidden feather. She failed even to reprove him. He seized the chance—he put the curling thing into his mouth, and chewed the end of it experimentally. He spit it out in disgust. He sat down again in her lap, and began playing with the frogs on her new coat. He fingered the interesting fringe. He squirmed about more vigorously than ever. He called to her. He put his hands up to her face. She bent down and kissed him, but not as she usually gathered him against herself with warmth. The caress was hard and preoccupied, and he whispered a little. He tried pat-a-caking, to get her to smile upon him. That, too, failed. Wully handed him the whip, and he shook it so fiercely that they had both hastily to rescue their faces from the blows he might have inflicted. Still his mother looked straight ahead.

They came then to a low place. The horses could go only very slowly. The baby adjusted himself to the new motion of the wagon. There was a splashing of mud that made him giggle delightedly. It would have been a choice morning for any baby whose mother wasn't sitting frozen. Wee Johnnie made the best of it. He kicked, and giggled, and squirmed about.

The horses failed of their own accord to take their proper pace again. Wully had to speak to them. He slapped them lightly with the lines.

"Get up, Nellie!" he exclaimed. "What's the matter of you?"

Wee Johnnie moved his arms exactly as Wully had done.

"Get up, Nellie!" he said. "What's the matter of you?"

He said all that, plainly, if not perfectly, and before he knew what was happening, his mother had seized him, and was hugging him up against her, in the good old way, kissing him.

"Get up, Nellie!" he cooed. "What's the matter of you!"

She had been so surprised, so delighted with her son's first sentence that she had turned, even kissing him, to Wully, no joy complete unless he shared it.

"Did you hear that!" she cried triumphantly, her face blossoming towards him. "Say it again, Lammie!"

And almost before Wully could smile in return, he stopped. He turned around. He thought he heard a groan from his load. He couldn't even smile at her with that man possibly spying upon them. He looked—and from the end of the wagon that man had lifted his head a little, like a snake, and had seen the smile that Chirstie had turned upon her husband. And Wully—when he saw that face—it was the last thing in the world that he intended doing—but some way, in spite of himself, he achieved generosity—the spoil, it may have been, of ancestral struggle. At the terrible sight of that face, he pitied his enemy. That coward, in his damned way, had loved Chirstie. And in his tormented sunken dying he had seen all the sweet intimacy from which he had been shut out and had sunk back, felled by the blow of that revelation. Wully had foregone revenge. He had forborne running a sword less sharp through his fallen enemy than Chirstie's wifely smile had been. In a flash Wully saw himself sitting there by the woman, loved, living, not dying, full of strength and generations, while that man, loathed and rejected, was already burning in hell.

The poor devil!

He pulled the horses up suddenly, and gave his wife the lines. He climbed back to lift his cousin into a position less painful. Through holes in the old blanket, straws from beneath were scratching the ghastly face. There was a farmhouse not so far down the road.

"I'll stop there and buy him a pillow," Wully resolved.

Margaret Wilson – A Concise Bibliography

Novels

The Able McLaughlins (1923)
The Kenworthys (1925)
The Painted Room (1926), sequel to The Kenworthys
Daughters of India (1928)
Trousers of Taffeta (1929)
The Dark Duty (1931)
The Valiant Wife (1933)
The Law and the McLaughlins (1936), sequel to The Able McLaughlins

Novel for Children

The Devon Treasure Mystery (1939)

Non-Fiction

The Crime of Punishment (1931)